WARZONE

THE ALEX HOLST FILES

AMRYN CROSS

REICHENBACH PRESS

For information **www.theeeastwind.amryncross.com**

Cover design by Brandon Daniel **www.brandondanielart.com/**

Author photo by Lisa Smith and LHS Photography
www.lhsphotography.com/

ISBN: 1500784990

First Edition: January 2015

Praise for WARZONE

"Loved the interaction between these characters. They stumped one another, built one another up, played off each other, and made me want more."

"Warzone is a great read. Alex, the heroine, is a cross between Sherlock Holmes and Bones. Her lack of social skills and her brilliance along with a sense of innocence make her an intriguing character. Cade, the hero, is a strong, yet damaged, military man. His imperfections endear him to the reader."

"I love the way neither of them really fits in anywhere, except with each other."

CHAPTER ONE

Sometimes when he closed his eyes, Cade Blackwell still saw the war. Times like now, that seemed preferable to the eyes wide open, put on a smile approach to civilian life.

When he did open his eyes after a long pause—probably too long if he really thought about it—his old friend Tim Moore still sat in front of him at the outdoor café.

"It's so good to see you," Tim insisted for not the first time since they'd run into each other on the DC Mall. "Can't believe it's been, what, fifteen years? We're getting old, man."

Cade forced a tight smile then chugged the coffee he hadn't wanted but felt compelled to order because Tim insisted on paying. When the empty paper cup began to shake in his right hand, he hastily returned it to the table. Maybe Tim wouldn't notice.

"So what are you doing now? Working? Kids?" It seemed

Tim wouldn't take a hint. "I don't see a ring so I guess you're still a bachelor, huh? Or maybe divorced."

Great observation. "Yeah, I haven't really had much time for dating." Or ridiculous coffee drinks with people he hadn't seen since medical school. "Congrats on your family, though. I heard you were a doctor down at Georgetown, so that's…great."

Ugh. Could he sound any lamer? That bit of information had come courtesy of the Google searches Cade had performed on his former classmates in his search for a place to live. Dr. Tim Moore—married with three kids—had been one of his last hopes. At least life was still moving forward for other people. He wasn't bitter. Not at all.

"Yeah, yeah, I'm the chief of anesthesiology." Tim chuckled and rubbed his index finger against the gray in his beard. "I teach students how to put people to sleep."

He definitely knew how.

"You joined the army, right?" Tim took another slow sip of his coffee—not black like Cade had ordered, but some mocha sugary syrup thing. "I remember you walking around campus in your uniform with a parade of girls behind you."

Of course that's how he would remember it. Never mind they'd made plans to finish medical school together, work at the same hospital after Cade returned from his tour of duty. Cade had been in the ROTC program, put in the hours of PT and special courses to prepare himself in every way possible to live his dream as an army officer, a trauma surgeon.

He still had nightmares but no M.D. after his name to show for it.

"Yeah, I just recently got out. I'm back in DC for a while." He found it easier to talk if he didn't look directly at Tim. Over his shoulder was good. Lots of people watching in downtown DC.

"You got out? I thought you were a lifer?"

Cade worried his bottom lip between his teeth as he contemplated an answer. This was exactly why he didn't like having social hour with old friends. He couldn't answer this question without explaining his forced retirement, which he couldn't explain without his injury, which he couldn't explain without saying that yes, he had watched half his platoon die that day and had been unable to save most of the injured. That always shut people up, but not before he'd inhaled the memories of smoke-filled lungs, the hail of bullets, and the dampness of the cave where he'd awaited rescue.

He closed his eyes and saw it again.

This wasn't normal.

"Cade? You okay?"

Obviously not, but they couldn't sit there in silence forever. "Yeah, sorry. I, uh, was injured in an IED explosion in Afghanistan. Got sent home about three months ago and handed my retirement papers."

"Retirement? You're a lucky man. I'm still paying for med school."

Yes, the moral of that story absolutely was that Cade was a lucky man. Never mind he'd almost died, and the only thing he knew how to do had been ripped from him. The fingers of his right hand, which he'd hidden beneath the table, dug into his thigh in an effort to keep from punching his former friend. Maybe he should just knock himself out.

Tim remained oblivious. "Weren't you going to join the medical corps anyway? I thought those guys didn't see much action. Just stitching up some bullet holes, right?"

Cade was saved an assault charge by a sharp cry and sudden movement over Tim's left shoulder. A man darted from the small crowd at full speed with a small package in his hand. People pulled out their cell phones or pointed, but not a single person moved to stop him.

Instinct took over, and Cade's legs had him half-way across the street at a sprint before his mind caught up with him. He'd just finished a three mile run around the Mall when he met Tim, but the stiffness in his joints wasn't enough to slow him down. Eyes locked on his target, he adjusted his angle to put himself in optimum position to intercept the mugger.

The kid—he couldn't have been over nineteen—who had been looking over his shoulder as he ran, came to an abrupt halt as he crashed into Cade. They both fell to the sidewalk, and Cade scolded himself for not setting his feet properly. The package was easy enough to rip away from the frightened teen, who then jumped up and disappeared into the crowd empty-handed.

The adrenaline rush barely registered on his radar and was completely gone by the time Cade got to his feet. In its tiny wake, it left the taste of dissatisfaction in his mouth. He examined the brown paper package. This wasn't about him.

No one approached him as he tucked the package under his left arm and jogged the couple hundred feet to where Tim was now assisting the woman who'd been robbed. The ring of onlookers began to disperse, barely fazed by the mugging. So much for chivalry.

The woman seemed strangely subdued considering she had a nasty cut on her forearm, which was bleeding through the stack of napkins Tim had pressed to it. Other than that, nothing marked her as a victim. No tears, her chin tipped high and her expression almost bored as Tim readjusted her makeshift bandage.

"Cade, there you are." Tim breathed an audible sigh of relief as Cade approached. Seemed like he was still as uncomfortable with conscious patients as ever. No wonder he'd become an anesthesiologist. "A-are you okay?"

Cade followed Tim's eyes to see his right hand trembled violently. He barely even noticed the sensation anymore, but it hadn't been that bad since after he woke up in the base hospital. He tried to clamp his fingers into a fist, but his grip was weak. Great. This was definitely not the time for an episode. Just keep it together long enough to make a clean exit.

"Yeah, it's just, you know, a side effect of my injury."

Tim eyed him with genuine concern. "Still, it wasn't shaking so bad a few minutes ago. You should let me look at it."

"I don't—"

"Doctor's orders. Besides, I'm taking 007 here to my office so I can stitch her up." He glanced over his shoulder at the woman who returned his quip with a sullen glare, intensified by the light color of her eyes. "We had such a good streak going. No stitches in six months and then this."

She lifted the napkins to examine the cut on her arm, then replaced them with a slight grimace. "Mostly white collar crimes in the last few months. You hardly need stitches for a paper cut."

Though her fine features and ivory skin spoke of delicacy, this woman's voice had a rich velvet smoothness. Nothing like the fine china her face brought to mind.

Cade found her pretty in a very striking sort of way, the sort that he didn't know what to do with. Waves of raven black hair must have fallen from her ponytail during the attack, and they now framed her pale face and set off her unusual eyes. Unusual not only for their light gray-green color, but the sharpness with which they studied him.

"Well, you definitely need stitches for that," Tim insisted. "C'mon, both of you. My car's just around the way."

Twenty minutes later, Cade found himself in a small room in the basement of MedStar Georgetown University Hospital, still holding the woman's package and still wondering why he'd agreed to come along. He was fine, really. The shaking in his hand had calmed considerably to his usual more subtle tremor.

But what else was he going to do? Wasn't like he had anything or anyone to go home to, and Tim had already seen his hand so there was no use hiding it. He'd wanted to reconnect with society, and God had presented him with an opportunity, though not one he particularly wanted.

The woman perched on the edge of a table and tossed the blood-soaked napkins down beside her. He took that opportunity to approach her while Tim gathered the supplies for stitches.

"I held on to this for you." Cade set the small square box on the table beside her. Awkward silence bloomed in the space between them. Awkward on his part anyway. She just gave him a once-over then turned her attention to Tim.

Really? He'd just tackled a guy for her, and she couldn't even look at him. He knew most people found him a little gruff, but some manners wouldn't kill her. "Well, you could say thank you."

"Yes, I could if you hadn't just blown my bust of a smuggling ring," she fired back without looking at him.

Tim rejoined them with a half smile in Cade's direction and a knowing shake of his head.

"I'm sorry. What?" Cade tilted his head and stared at this strange creature in front of him.

She sighed as if she were put out with him and finally gave Cade her full attention. The intensity reminded him of staring into the sun. "Admittedly, I hadn't counted on any heroes being present. I've watched that spot for weeks and no one even bats an eye when someone yells. Trust me, I've tried it. Nice tackle, though."

The corner of his mouth twitched up before he could suppress the disbelieving smile. Who was this girl?

"She's always like this," Tim assured him as he placed his tools on the table and pulled on some gloves. After briefly examining the wound, he reached for a syringe.

"No, not the lidocaine. I told you that doesn't work on me." She pursed her lips slightly.

Tim shook his head. "It's all you're getting from me. So it's this or nothing."

A terse huff ruffled the hair around her face. "Nothing then. I can always use more data on the human body's pain responses."

Unbelievable. Cade allowed himself a quick glance around the room to check for hidden cameras. Surely someone was playing a joke on him. He'd given his fair share of stitches to soldiers without the benefit of lidocaine, but this girl didn't look like a soldier. But Tim didn't seem the least bit surprised by her behavior.

"So, we didn't officially meet," he began. After his first attempt to speak to her, it would probably be better to leave well enough alone. But some part of him couldn't resist poking the cage. Besides, he didn't want to watch Tim botch these stitches when he knew good and well he could do them better himself. Well, could have done before his injury. "I'm Cade Blackwell."

"The name's Alexandria Holst, and you may call me Alex. Not Allie, not Lexi, but Alex." She spoke so quickly he had to strain to keep up. Like a sports car on a road course, she navigated the language with a precision and speed yet unmatched in his experience. "Pleased to meet you, Cade Blackwell."

And for the breadth of a second, she *did* look pleased to meet him, though the flash of a smile was so quick he almost missed it.

"Nice to meet you, too, Alex. How do you know Tim?"

"He keeps me supplied in chemicals," she stated matter-of-factly. "Or he used to. Now he's pawned the job off on one of the pathology residents."

"She means I delegated," Tim said from his hunched position over her arm.

"Nope, I meant pawned."

"Right." Tim tied off the thread and cut it close to her skin before covering his handiwork with a bandage. There would be a scar, Cade was sure of it. "There, good as new. You didn't even flinch."

Cade had forgotten she'd opted out of the anesthetic. Impressive.

"Of course not." She hopped off the table and smoothed her shirt.

He expected her to make a quick exit, but Alex shoved the package in her jacket pocket and made a show of examining the shelf full of specimen jars along the opposite wall, clearly in no hurry to leave.

"How's your hand?" Unfortunately Tim hadn't forgotten about his promise to look Cade over. "You must've had a pretty nasty fall."

"Not the fall," Alex singsonged from across the small room, her back still to both of them. "Obviously the head injury."

Cade froze, which only made the trembling of his right hand in his pocket that much more obvious. How could she know about that?

"Was it Afghanistan? I'll bet it was Afghanistan." She whirled to face him, just the hint of a smirk on her pretty face. "Just recently back, aren't you?"

"Yes," he practically whispered before clearing his throat. What use was there in denying it? "Three months. How did you know?"

Alex smiled, but not the sort that seemed real. She walked a circle around him as she talked, eyes traveling up and down.

"How do I know you're an army officer—likely medical—recently returned from Afghanistan? And that you suffered an injury which diminished your peripheral vision and gave you an intermittent tremor in your right hand?"

He blinked. Once, twice, but said nothing. Forming words seemed impossible.

"I see it. Your posture gives you away as military immediately, as well as your hair which is currently growing out of the close cropped style. Your hands and face are tan, but your forearms are lighter suggesting you've been in the sun but also fully covered. Your hand, obviously is shaking slightly, and you would've never been allowed to carry a gun with a tremor like that, therefore it's a recent development. You're still in immaculate shape, so you haven't been relegated to a desk. That suggests you're retired. The clench in your jaw just now suggests you don't like it. Your peripheral vision on your right side is poor, which I know because as I walked around you, you shifted slightly in that direction to get a better look at me, while when I was on your left, you remained perfectly still. And I say medical corps because you think Tim did a poor job on my stitches—quite correct on that one, but I don't care about a scar."

And there it was. All out in the open for everyone to see. It didn't feel like he'd imagined it would. His heart tattooed the familiar beat of excitement against his chest as he refused to look away from her confident gaze.

"Amazing." He finally breathed out the word bouncing around his brain. For a brief moment, she seemed startled with widened eyes, though recovered quickly.

For the first time in three months, he wasn't thinking about his injury, about his therapy sessions, or about the nightmares. His brain simply couldn't process anything beyond how incredible her assessment of him was. Like she'd seen right past the "normal" face he'd tried to put on. Even if he wanted to be angry, he couldn't.

"I probably should've warned you about her." Tim was the only one who seemed slightly uncomfortable. He looked between Cade and Alex. "She's done that to everybody here at one time or another. Hard to keep secrets around her."

Hard to lie, he probably meant. There was something refreshing about everything stripped bare. No pretending. Not everyone would like that.

"Well, I have to be going," Alex announced with a quick glance around the room. "Tim, I hope we don't see each other again for a while."

Cade swallowed the snicker that bubbled up in his throat. Rude but amusing. "I'll walk out with you," he offered. "Tim, it was nice to see you again. "

"You too, buddy." He clapped Cade on the back and held out his hand for a shake. "See you around."

He had to jog to catch up with Alex down the basement hallway. She slowed slightly when he fell into step beside her, and that alone struck him as odd. First impressions being what they were, she'd seemed annoyed with him at best. Probably hadn't expected him to have the guts to force his presence on her, yet, she'd made a tiny concession to allow it.

"Were you really trying to take down a smuggling ring?" he

asked. It sounded preposterous when she first mentioned it, but after that display, he was prepared to believe almost anything about her.

"Yes." Her tone remained as expressionless as her face when she looked over to study him. "I'd been working on it for several months. There was a GPS tracker in that box, which would have tracked the route the boy took to bring it back to his employer. Lots of reconnaissance went into that planning, all for you to ruin it."

"You shouldn't have called for help if you didn't want it," he pointed out as they pushed through an exit door and onto a busy sidewalk.

"Right. Because it's not suspicious if someone mugs you and you just stand there and watch." Hands in her pockets, she looked left, right, anywhere but directly at him. "No, it had to look convincing."

"It was definitely convincing."

"Then at least something went right, but it hardly makes up for losing that lead."

Was she hinting that she wanted him to make it up to her? Like a date? Nothing she'd said or done so far had given him that impression, but clearly her words were meant to evoke a response.

"You're staying at the transitional housing at the VA, aren't you?" Her eyes squinted against the sun to finally find his.

"Do I want to ask how you knew that?"

"You're a veteran recently returned from the war with an injury. A head injury at that. You've only recently been released from inpatient therapy so that's not enough time to find other living arrangements. Leaving the city isn't appealing to you, but there's no way you can afford a place to yourself on your army pension. I imagine you're looking for a roommate."

"That's amazing." Apparently that's the only word his brain could wrap itself around when she spoke. "I hadn't told anyone."

She opened her mouth as if to speak, but closed it quickly, leaving him insatiably curious what had almost passed her lips. Another quick scan of their surroundings, then her eyes returned to him. "I know a place in Stanton Park. A nice place in the middle of everything. It's pricy, but I know the landlady who lives in the downstairs apartment so she'll give me a good price. Still, it would be much more affordable with a roommate."

He waited for the question, but it never came. Just assumed. "Sorry, did you just ask me to live with you?" She was crazy. "We don't even know each other."

"I'm sure if you give me just a minute I can recite a few more details of your life history if that's what you're interested in. Otherwise, just consider this me collecting my favor for your involvement with the smugglers."

"I didn't offer to do you a favor."

"Well, you should have. I've been told that's good manners." She somehow managed to ooze enough charm that he forgot why it sounded so absurd. "Stanton Park area. Constitution Avenue and 10th tomorrow at one. If you don't like it, you're free to walk away." And then, with no further goodbye, she did just that.

Cade laughed and rubbed the back of his neck as people pushed by him on the sidewalk. Even after more than a decade in the military, Alex Holst may have been the strangest thing to have ever happened to him. Unfortunately, walking away had never been his strong suit.

CHAPTER TWO

He dreamed about the war again.

The nightmares weren't every night, and in the respites Cade forgot just how terrifying they actually were. But tonight he'd woken up with a gasp on his lips and tears in his eyes.

The numbers on his watch glowed 2:17. He sat up and cradled his head in his hands. For a brief moment that afternoon, he'd felt almost normal—though probably because Alex was just so abnormal by comparison—and had forgotten his reality was much different.

Sleep wouldn't find him again tonight. He knew that from experience. With a resigned sigh, he threw his legs over the side of the hard bed and planted them on the carpet below. His morning routine wouldn't start for another four hours.

Morning run, breakfast, therapy session, roommate/cheap housing search, maybe pick up a few groceries. The same almost every day since he'd been released to live on his own. Tim and Alex had interrupted that. Well, mostly Alex. She'd been a disturbingly bright spot in an otherwise gray haze, and she'd offered a solution to the roommate problem.

He didn't like the idea of living with a woman. His dating experience had provided him with more than enough theoretical reasons why even if he'd never moved in with any of his girlfriends. Things were bound to get messy.

But he couldn't dismiss the idea. A cheap room in the Capitol Hill area of DC was hard to come by. Only a fool wouldn't give it a second thought. Besides, it couldn't be any worse than army barracks. So far, he'd been unable to come up with anyone he'd previously known to room with. At least he'd met Alex once, so it wasn't like rooming with a complete stranger.

Except it was. Because she'd told him everything about him but nothing about herself. Remarkable. If he hadn't known better, he'd have dismissed her generalizations and stereotypes outright, but she'd been right about all of it, even his silent critique of Tim's stitching ability.

He grabbed his phone from the small nightstand and typed her name into the search engine. Graduated Johns Hopkins in 2004 with a master's degree in chemistry, making her around 34 in his estimation, though he'd have thought a bit younger. A link to her master's thesis, which consisted of a bunch of words he couldn't pronounce but seemed to be about cataloging the subtle difference in soil samples from the DC and Baltimore area.

The second page of links led him to a letter she'd written

while she was still at Johns Hopkins to the *International Journal of Criminal Investigation*. The limited utility of forensic science in timely apprehension of unknown suspects. A quick scan of the article revealed she'd suggested investigators relied too heavily on modern forensic science, which was notoriously slow and fraught with errors. Careful observation of crime scenes, victims, and suspects would provide immediate leads, which would result in quicker arrests, which could then be confirmed with the science that would hold up in court.

Cade shook his head. As a college freshman, she'd been telling investigators world-wide how to do their jobs. It sounded preposterous, but the journal *had* published the letter. And after the demonstration he'd witnessed at the hospital, he was inclined to believe her. Either she was the real thing or an excellent fake.

He was beyond intrigued. Enough that by the time the sun rose above the DC skyline, he'd decided to show up for the meeting after all.

The Stanton Park neighborhood seemed miles from DC though he could still see the Congressional Library's dome and its crowning golden torch as he stepped from the Eastern Market Metro station. It looked more like small town USA with a CVS, a small public library, and a few local shops lining the streets. Seemed an odd place for Alex to want to call home. Cade couldn't imagine many smuggling rings based their operations in Stanton Park.

Still, he'd made up his mind to meet her and see what this was all about. A look at his watch confirmed he had plenty of time to stroll to his destination, so he headed up 7th street, in front of the Eastern Market and past several locals enjoying their lunches on outdoor patios. Despite his misgivings about the quaintness of the area, the tree-lined streets and Victorian rowhouses had a certain charm about them. Maybe he could actually relax here. He didn't always have to be in the thick of things.

Even as he thought it, the falseness of that statement pinged against his conscience. The old Cade, the one who'd left for war with his naïve vision of the American Dream, would've loved it here. The neighborhood was convenient to Capitol Hill, so all sorts of chaos was just a Metro ride away.

Cade reached the corner of Constitution and 10th just as a cab pulled to the curb. The door opened and Alex appeared, wearing much the same thing as he'd seen her in the day before—dark trousers, simple shirt, and a trench coat tailored within an inch of its life. He felt severely underdressed in his jeans, t-shirt, and jacket.

"I knew you'd show up." She smiled and buttoned two of the buttons on her coat.

"No, you didn't."

"Of course I did. You'd be an idiot not to show up, and while most people *are* idiots, you seem to be of above average intelligence."

"Thanks." *I think.* "So which house is it?"

"1221. Follow me."

They strolled past several homes with no small talk before Alex came to a stop in front of a gray Victorian townhouse with two front doors. Alex's eyes flickered to the one that sat atop the brick stairs, but she moved to the one just three steps down from ground level instead. "Mrs. Turner is expecting us. I told her a bit about you. Hope you don't mind."

As if he had a choice. He stood behind Alex as she knocked at the door. Seconds later, it opened to reveal an older lady, probably in her seventies, with gray hair bobbed to her chin and sparkling blue eyes.

"Alex," she cooed as she pulled the younger woman into a quick embrace. "I haven't seen you in a few days."

"Working, Mrs. Turner," Alex mumbled as she stepped inside and brushed her coat off. "This is Cade Blackwell, the soldier I was telling you about."

"Oh, a handsome fellow." Mrs. Turner's smile reminded him of a proud grandmother. Behind her, Alex turned to look him over as if she hadn't noticed what he looked like. Considering the clinical distance with which she'd analyzed him, she probably hadn't. Noting his dark blond hair and light brown eyes probably didn't offer her much in the way of information.

"Pleased to meet you, Mrs. Turner." He returned the older lady's smile with one of his own, though much more hesitant and cautious. *Remember to be nice, act normal.*

"Oh, call me Edith, please." She motioned him inside and shut the door behind them. "Would you like something to drink?"

"No, I'm fine, thank you." Yes, good with the manners. Mrs. Turner—Edith—was easier to talk to than most people he'd encountered since his return from the war. Maybe because she didn't know anything about him, or it could have been the sense that it wouldn't have mattered to her anyway.

"All right then. I guess Alex can show you around. I'm afraid I don't do the stairs much anymore because of my hip. That's why I moved to the downstairs apartment."

"Thank you," he forced, but only slightly. So much easier to converse with strangers than people who'd known him before the war. They had no expectation of how he should be, and if they didn't like him, he just wrote it off as a misunderstanding between civilian and soldier.

"No, thank *you*. I don't like for this place to be so empty, and Alex is so rarely here. I've been looking for someone to look after things, especially since I'll be leaving in a few days to visit my grandchildren. Do you want to see pictures? I have lots…" She wrung her hands slightly as her eyes danced between Alex and him. Cade suspected Edith was used to serving people and didn't know what to do with her hands when she wasn't. He certainly understood that feeling.

There. Take that, Alex. It wasn't so hard to make generalizations about people. Not so impressive after all.

"Some other time." Alex saved him having to answer. "This way, Cade." Short and to the point. He was sensing a pattern with her.

The stairs from the entry to Edith's apartment led up to a second level open floor space with old wood flooring and neutral gray and white walls. Alex insinuated herself into one of the two worn chairs framing the fireplace and watched his reaction.

"Very nice," he couldn't help saying. The house was obviously old, but he liked that about it. Small living room, but enough to fit those two chairs, a couch against the far wall and, impossibly, in the little corner by the stairs, a piano. It already felt more like a home than his quarters at the VA.

"We could lose the couch if you have furniture, but I'm afraid this chair and that piano are non-negotiable," Alex informed him, her fingers drumming against the armrests of her chair.

"These are your things? Did you already move in?" Was she really so sure of him that she'd agreed to take the place?

She shrugged. "I saw an opportunity. And no, most of this was Mrs. Turner's furniture, but I brought the piano with me, and I've appropriated this chair. Good for thinking. You can have the other one."

"The other one" was a faded burgundy color that clashed defiantly with the burnt orange fabric of the chair Alex occupied. If his mother could see this, she'd throw a fit at the lack of consideration for coordinating decor. Cade sort of liked it. In fact, each piece of furniture seemed to have been orphaned from its original set, but instead of looking odd or out of place in the room, the uniqueness of each one made it feel more comfortable.

"And the rest of the house?" he asked once he stopped admiring the hodge-podge furniture. Alex was supposed to be showing him around, not studying him with those keen eyes.

"Kitchen through there, two bedrooms upstairs, two bathrooms. Nice little patio out back." Alex waved her hand in the direction of each feature, but never moved from her chair. If anything, she sunk further into it.

"That's it?"

She frowned, light gray-green eyes disappearing under her black lashes. "What else do you need?"

"No, I mean, you're not going to show it to me?"

"Does it matter?" She stood, her heels clicking on the wood floor as she strolled to the window and looked out. Cade knew what she would see—quiet tree-lined streets—and wondered again why she'd chosen this house. "You're not worried about the accommodations. You're more concerned about having me as a roommate. So go ahead, ask your questions."

True, the accommodation itself wasn't a concern. The house was plenty spacious, and it sounded like he'd have his own bedroom and bathroom, so they'd only share the kitchen and living area. Definitely better than army barracks. Alex was the definite question mark, but where did he start? "Mrs. Turner said you weren't home much."

"It's mostly true." Turning away from the window, her eyes fixed him in place, not because she scared or intimidated him, but because he hoped if he studied her long enough, he might be able to see the wheels turning behind those unusual eyes. "Cases take me all over the city at all hours. Can't ever predict when I might be here. But don't mind me. You'll hardly know I'm here. Just the occasional piano playing when I need to think."

"Cases." Yes, she'd mentioned something about those yesterday. She didn't look like any police officer he'd ever seen, so maybe she was federal? "What sort of cases?"

"You know, the usual. Theft, smuggling, murders, extortion." A dark smile teased her lips, and he shifted uncomfortably under the weight of it. "But not the boring ones.

Only the really good ones. I don't bother with drug deals gone bad and all that. But a really good poisoning or apparent suicide? Those are like Christmas."

A faint alarm went off in the back of his mind. What was wrong with her? And what was wrong with him that he was considering living with a person who smiled like that when talking about murders? A small swell of tension knotted in his gut.

"I looked you up last night," he confessed.

"I would have been disappointed if you hadn't."

"I read your letter to the *International Journal of Criminal Investigation*. That was... bold of you."

"It's not bold when you're always right."

"And you're always right?"

"Was I wrong about anything I said about you?" She maintained a respectable distance, but there was something intimate in her gaze. A reminder that there was no use hiding anything from her. He hated that he *liked* that about her. Slowly, the knot in his stomach worked itself loose.

He cleared his throat. "No. But that can't work on everyone."

She just smiled.

It couldn't, right? Crap. Maybe it did. Now he was more intrigued.

"So you're just what? A private detective?"

Her smile slipped away, and her serious façade took its place. "Consulting detective, actually. I have...connections with the police in town. They come to me when they're at a loss, which is almost always."

So either she was delusional, or he was getting in over his head. There was something dangerously attractive about each option.

"I'm going to finish looking around," he announced to buy himself some time. This was crazy, all of it, but coming home from the war had taught him that his new "normal" would drive him insane. Maybe he'd be better off with a little crazy. Besides, if he couldn't find cheap housing, he'd have to leave the city, and he wasn't sure he could bear to be anywhere else.

He walked into the kitchen—small with just a breakfast table—and perused the space. Not a lot of frills, but he didn't mind. There was a pantry against the far wall and a refrigerator. He pulled open the fridge door to survey the contents. A couple apples, a carton of Chinese takeout that looked like it might have been in there too long, and a bottle of ketchup.

Alex's heels clicked like machine gun fire before she appeared in the kitchen. "Sorry about—"

She cut herself off just as he looked up from the door.

"What?"

"Oh. Nothing. Never mind," she replied innocently. Too innocently.

"No, you don't just run into a room and yell sorry and not have a reason."

She cocked her head, as if she'd never considered that. "I thought I left an experiment in the fridge."

"Unless you mean the decades old Chinese, I think you're okay." Cade shut the door. "Maybe we can alternate the grocery shopping? We'll definitely need some basics—milk, eggs, bread..."

"Oh, I rarely eat when I'm on a case."

O...kay. But she had to eat some time, right? "Are you on a case right now?"

A wrinkle formed between her eyebrows with her serious frown. The small line between her brows suggested she did a lot of that. "Are you... are you asking me to dinner?"

"No, I wasn't—"

"Because I'm flattered, but I'm really not interested. Not that there's anything wrong with you, of course—other than the head injury, I mean—but the work really does take all my time."

"I wasn't asking you out." He ground out the words through nearly clenched teeth once she finally stopped to take a breath. Cade didn't know whether to be offended or laugh. No woman had ever been quite so direct with him.

"Oh." Alex's lips pursed as she squinted at him, complete with a slight tilt of her head. As if she'd had occasion to use that line several times, but Cade hadn't followed the script. Twice in five minutes he seemed to have given her pause. "Well, that's fine then."

"Of course it's fine. I don't date roommates."

"I should hope not. Now, for the case." She switched gears fast enough to give him whiplash. "I've been asked to attend a meeting with Nathan Bishop—a member of the clergy and a staff member of the Chaplain of the House. Would you like to come along?"

Cade blinked at her. "Me?"

"You should get out." She left the kitchen and retrieved her black coat from the back of her chair. He followed her almost involuntarily. "You asked me if my methods always work. I'm offering you a chance to watch. Unless of course you'd rather just sit around here."

Of course he didn't want to just sit around. He'd spent the last three months doing just that. It was time for a change. Of course, in the last five minutes, he'd apparently moved in with female roommate who solved crimes for a living. Maybe there was such a thing as too much change.

"But then again," she continued as she slid the coat on and fastened two of the buttons, "you were a soldier. If you've seen your share of excitement in the war, maybe you should stay here."

"I was a combat medic," he corrected quietly.

She paused and narrowed her eyes slightly. Probably filing that bit of information away somewhere. "Still, you've certainly earned the right to relax for a while. Take it easy."

She wielded her words like a scalpel, dissecting him and peeling back the layers. He could feel it but couldn't do anything about it except take the bait. "I'm coming."

CHAPTER THREE

"So people just call you up when they have a problem?" Cade was still trying to work out the logistics of her business as they exited a cab near… well, he wasn't sure what they were near. Alex had spent the entire ride captivating him with tales of her various cases. If anything, his admiration for her had only grown as he got lost both literally and figuratively in her stories.

"Text and email mostly. That way I can weed out the complete idiots before I waste my time."

"What sort of things do people hire you for?" He was imagining a film noir private detective but then realized it would probably take Alex half a second to determine if someone's spouse was cheating or associated with the mafia. What kind of cases landed in the lap of someone so intelligent?

"Extortion, blackmail, missing persons. You name it and I've probably solved it." There wasn't any sort of pride in her voice, just a clinical statement of fact. "A lot of my work comes from the police though. Those are the really good ones. Serial killers, terrorist threats, bank robberies."

"And what does Nathan Bishop want to hire you for?" In retrospect, he probably should have asked before they left the house so he'd have some idea what he was walking into. The soldier in him chided him for being so reckless. Reckless got people hurt.

"No idea," she replied as she stopped in front of a stone building, which appeared to be no more than one story but stretched out like a lazy yawn across two blocks. Maybe some sort of parsonage or offices that connected to the adjacent church. "Let's go see."

She executed one sharp knock against the door, which pushed open under her hand. Her lips twitched subtly into a mischievous smirk as amusement sparked in her eyes.

His response was much more visceral. Something in the air had shifted, and despite Alex's comments on his visual impairment, everything appeared in sharp focus. The sort of clear calmness that came over him before battle.

Alex stepped forward. He clamped a hand around her arm without thinking and pulled her back from the door. Something felt very wrong, and he'd learned not to question his instincts when it came to something like this.

"Let go," she insisted with a hint of something other than annoyance in her voice.

He complied, but did his best to fix her in place with a stare. "Something's not right in there."

Her lips flattened to a straight line as her eyes searched his. "Maybe he just unlocked the door because he was expecting us."

"You don't believe that."

"Of course not." She scoffed and actually smiled. "And that's what makes this so much fun."

Stopping her was out of the question as she was already inside the door before he could finish blinking. He made the choice to follow her just as quickly. Letting her walk into danger alone wasn't an option. Even if his conscience would allow it, his military training wouldn't. Never leave a man behind.

The door opened to a small foyer with exposed stone walls and lots of dark decor. From the entry stretched a long hall with several closed doors on either side. That's all Cade managed to take in before the man sprinting down the hallway stole his attention.

"Help! Help!" As he neared, Cade could see the look of terror on the man's face. Tears streaked his red face and something crimson stained his right hand.

Cade reached for his gun before he realized it wasn't there, but Alex remained perfectly still as the man approached them.

"Thank God," he panted, latching on to Alex's sleeve with wide eyes. She leaned back to distance herself, but didn't immediately pull her arm away. "You're the police, aren't you? Tell me you're the police."

Cade looked left toward Alex, then internally reviewed his own clothing choices. Nothing should have made this man suspect they were the police.

"Have you called the police?" Alex sounded calm. Too calm.

"No, but—"

"Then why would we be the police?"

The man froze, hand trembling where it fisted in the material of her coat, then slowly backed away. Fortunately for him, Alex's coat remained unstained. "Y-you're not them?"

"We were—" Cade began.

"We're here to investigate," Alex interrupted as she not so subtly jammed him in the side with her elbow. "What can you tell us?"

At the mention of an investigation, the man seemed to have forgotten his fears about them not being the police. "He's dead. Oh, Reverend Bishop is dead!" Then he buried his head in his hands and let out a wail.

Despite the theatrical display, Cade remained skeptical and on alert. He studied the closed doors and the hall behind the man. Too still. Still as death. Coupled with the apparent blood on the man's hand, it was enough to raise the hair on his neck.

"And you found him," Alex supplied with a touch of annoyance in her tone. "Yes, I gathered that much. When was the last time you saw Mr. Bishop alive?"

Though he was only half listening, Cade noted her refusal to use the title of reverend.

"About six this morning." The man sniffled and made an attempt to dry his eyes and throw his shoulders back. He must've decided this was an official police interview after all because he seemed to be doing his best to put on a brave face. It didn't help that he'd managed to wipe some blood across his cheek. "I stopped by for morning prayers and to revise the Reverend's sermon notes for this Sunday. Then I went out to make the final arrangements for our children's fundraiser this weekend, and when I came back I found him."

His voice trailed off in tears again, which prompted Alex to roll her eyes. Cade's mouth gaped. Couldn't she have the decency to not belittle the man to his face?

"Right." Her jaw clenched around the word. "Well, don't go wandering off. We'll need some time with the body."

Cade's eyes snapped to her. She looked completely serious. As much as he'd admired her stories in the cab, part of him thought maybe they were exaggerated. He certainly hadn't wanted to be part of one. Because that would be crazy… right?

"It's just that, no one else is here." The man's pleading face turned toward Alex, then back to Cade. "And I only just found him. How could the police get here so fast? Who called you?"

"It doesn't matter. What does matter is that you're impeding a murder investigation." Alex straightened her coat and sidestepped the man. "I suggest you go sit outside, maybe breathe into a paper bag, and stay out of the way. Someone will be along to question you further very soon."

Cade started to follow her down the hallway toward the only open door, but the man grabbed his arm to slow him down. With concerted self-control, Cade looked down into the terrified eyes of a man who'd just found someone he knew dead. A tiny bit of sympathy softened his heart. He knew what that was like.

"Are you really with the police?" he asked quietly. Presumably he was afraid of Alex hearing, though Cade suspected she was much too focused on the task at hand to concern herself with them.

But he couldn't lie, especially not here, in a church. He'd had a complicated relationship with religion since his childhood but had finally come to terms with God in Afghanistan. He was far from perfect, but lying had never been one of his vices.

"Sort of." Alex *did* say she worked with the police on several occasions.

The man's eyes widened and looked on the verge of another breakdown. Before he could witness it, Cade pulled his arm free and took off after Alex.

Surprisingly, she'd waited for him just outside the ajar door. They exchanged looks, Cade's one of stern caution and Alex's one of…well, it looked like complete bliss. But that couldn't be right.

"You heard him, right?" Cade glanced over his shoulder to make sure the hysterical man was out of earshot. "Because you're smiling."

"Yes." Her lips returned to their grin after her single word response.

"Maybe you could tone it down. It doesn't look good to be so happy when you learn someone has died."

"Smiling at crime scenes—not good. Right, I'll file that away." Just like that her smile morphed into a solemn mask. He couldn't tell if she was being sarcastic or genuinely naive. Hard to believe the latter could be true about her. "But just for the record, I have a good feeling about this one."

"Also not a great thing to say at a crime scene," he called after her, but she was already pushing against the door, and, he suspected, not paying any attention to him.

A putrid smell nearly knocked him down as he followed her into the next room. He swallowed hard against the bile and took a quick glance around. And immediately wished he hadn't.

The room, which appeared to be an office or study, looked to be in perfect order except for the dead man sitting in a chair pushed back from the desk. Beneath the desk, a crimson black pool of blood had formed. The man's head, which was slumped forward, and his shoulders were all that was visible with the desk in the way. Cade was content to leave it that way.

Alex didn't appear especially interested either. Her eyes trained on the floor, she walked seemingly aimless patterns before pausing in the middle of the room and closing her eyes.

He waited for her to say something, to react in some way, but she didn't oblige. Maybe this was just another weird manifestation of PTSD. He was hallucinating crime scenes. Maybe he was really asleep back at the VA.

Just to make sure, Cade bit the inside of his cheek so hard the metallic salt of blood mixed with his saliva. Not a great combination with the smell of a decaying body and sight of coagulating blood in front of him.

"That's it." He swallowed hard to make sure his lunch stayed down. "What are we doing here? I'm calling the police."

"We're here because Mr. Bishop asked for my services. He called me, not the police." Alex opened her eyes, but didn't look his direction.

"I'm pretty sure he didn't call you to investigate his own murder," Cade snapped, his eyes following her fluid movements around the room.

"Stranger things have happened," she practically hummed as she examined some mud near the door they'd entered moments before. "Now you can help me or you can stand there, but whatever you do, don't call the police."

"Don't call the police? What do you mean 'don't call the police'?" Obstruction of justice wasn't on his bucket list.

"I would have thought that was self-explanatory." Her voice remained frustratingly calm as she avoided his eyes, looking instead at the floor as she walked a seemingly random path around the room.

"There's a body in that chair over there!" He looked once, twice, to make sure it was still there. As if the man was going anywhere. "We *need* to call the police."

"A man is dead. There isn't time to call the police."

"Is this what you do? Hijack cases?" Cade squeezed the back of his neck until it hurt. Pain. Pain was good. Kept him grounded. "Did you know he was dead before we got here?"

She finally looked up at him and rolled her eyes so hard he thought she might sprain something. "I'm not psychic."

"No, of course not." The sarcasm was so thick, the words barely rolled off his tongue. What had he gotten himself in to?

"Oh, this is good." A hushed reverence clouded her words as she stooped to stare at something on one of the massive bookshelves lining the walls. "Cade, come here."

He did, slowly, cautiously, until she looked over her shoulder at him. "It's not booby-trapped. You could move a little quicker."

"I'm not worried about a booby-trap. I'm more concerned

that you're so happy about this."

"What's not to be happy about? Look at this. See, here on the shelf? What's missing?"

Nothing seemed to be missing. On the shelf she indicated, Bible commentaries, prayer journals, and biographies of martyrs were sandwiched so tightly it was hard to imagine removing one without pulling at least one other with it.

"They're jammed in there. Might be an extra book in there, but I can't see how something's missing."

"The dust," she breathed, prayer-like he would have said if she'd given any indication of being religious. "Look at the void around *The Works of Saint Augustine.* Someone's pulled that book out recently. You can put anything back except dust."

"But what does that tell us?" Did he just say 'us'? No, he shouldn't lump himself in with her. That could end badly.

As if on cue, voices rose in the hallway, and the faint howl of a police siren sounded from outside the building.

"I told him to wait." Alex groaned and moved away from the shelf, presumably referring to the hysterical aid they'd encountered on the way in. At least *someone* had enough sense to call the police.

The study's door shoved open, revealing a tall man with salt and pepper hair, dressed in a rumpled gray suit. His dark brows furrowed, nearly obscuring his eyes, though the annoyance was clear on his face. Understandable if he knew Alex.

"How many times have I told you not to start investigating without us?" the man asked as he crossed the room in a few long strides. A hint of desperation lined his words. He was frustrated, but not, apparently, with Alex's presence. Just her timing. "It looks bad."

"Hello to you, too, Detective Grisham." Alex flicked her eyes over the man, then turned her attention to straightening her coat. "And what looks bad is your team destroying half the useful evidence before you bother to call me. Besides, this is a good one."

The detective shook his head, but stopped when he finally seemed to notice Cade. Grisham's keen eyes gave him a once-over. "Who's this? A witness you've been interrogating?"

"This is my colleague, Captain Cade Blackwell," Alex interjected before Cade could answer. Just as well since he had no idea how to explain his presence there. Wait, had she just said 'captain'? He hadn't told her—

Grisham acknowledged him with a wary nod of his head. Cade couldn't blame him for embracing caution.

"You. What are you doing here?"

All eyes turned to the doorway. The gruff female voice entering the room belonged to a short red-head with a badge just in front of the gun on her hip. Unlike Grisham's exasperated entrance, this woman seemed genuinely angry at Alex's presence. Her small hands were clenched in white knuckled fists, and the fine lines around the corner of her mouth were accentuated by the tight purse of her lips.

"You've finally snapped, haven't you?" The woman's accusatory tone prickled the hair on the back of Cade's neck. As if things weren't tense enough with a body in their midst, the red-head had ratcheted things up another notch. "Killed the poor guy just to keep from being bored."

Alex inhaled slightly, and Grisham hung his head. Cade looked to the three people in the hostile triangle as he tried to wrap his mind around the words hanging between them. No one refuted the woman's accusation, but no one had moved to take Alex into custody. Worst of all, no one seemed surprised by the red head's words. Maybe there was more cause for concern than he'd originally thought. Even though Grisham didn't seem to want to act on the accusation, people didn't throw around words like that without a reason—exaggerated or not.

Finally, with her eyes still staring sharply at the other woman, Alex spoke. "Cade, this is Detective Sarah Walker. Big fan of mine as you can see."

He started to chuckle—his go-to nervous response—but bit it back when he saw all eyes on him. "Nice to meet you?"

It really wasn't supposed to come out like a question, but, based on that entrance, he was definitely doubtful about how nice anything about Sarah Walker was.

"You brought your boyfriend to a crime scene?" Sarah scoffed, hands finding their way to her hips. "I'm impressed the psychopath was able to find a date."

"Sociopath," Alex corrected at the time Cade said "Not her boyfriend."

Silence followed her declaration as Cade and the two detectives stared at her.

"What? Well, clearly I'm not a psychopath, which you'd know if you bothered to learn the difference—"

"That's enough, girls," Grisham thankfully interrupted with

a dart of his eyes in Cade's direction. As if to tell him he should get Alex under control. Boy, did he have another thing coming. "Sarah, get this place taped off before you let forensics or the medical examiner in here. Alex, take me through what you have so far."

Alex seemed oblivious to the glare Sarah gave her as she left the room, but he'd felt the daggers she shot at his roommate. Obviously some history between the two of them, but more one-sided than anything. He'd be willing to bet that with Alex, most things were one-sided. She hadn't shown a hint of emotional attachment to anything except her cases, and even then, not in the way he would've expected.

"Well, it's pretty obvious if you bother to look." Alex made a face, mocking a wince, as if it pained her to explain.

"Can we just skip the part where you assert your superior intelligence and cut right to the facts?" Grisham ignored her face and pulled a notebook from his jacket. "You've got five minutes before I have to let forensics in the room."

"Fine." She huffed and shoved her hands in her pockets. "The motive was obviously a robbery."

"I'm sorry, obviously?" Surely he hadn't heard her correctly. Cade had looked around the room the same as she had, and nothing seemed to be missing or even out of place. Except, of course, for the dust she'd seemed fascinated with.

Alex looked between him and Grisham, who subtly shrugged his slumped shoulders and raised his brows in Cade's direction. At least the detective seemed just as lost as Cade. "It must be nice to be so vacant. So much empty space in your heads.

Yes, *obviously* the motive was a robbery. However, the thieves weren't looking for money or valuables, at least not in the traditional sense. No, they wanted something specific."

She spun on her heels and walked to the door adjacent to Bishop's body—glass doors leading to a small garden/greenhouse. With her hand still in her pocket—to avoid leaving fingerprints?—Alex tried the handle. It didn't budge. She proceeded to do the same thing to the other two doors in the study, and they were both locked as well. Satisfied with her display, she faced them once again.

"All three doors—besides the main one—are locked. None of them tampered with. If these thieves were willing to kill a man for a robbery, they certainly wouldn't have qualms with breaking down a door or picking a lock to search for valuables. So either they knew what they were looking for was in this room, or, more likely, they knew they'd have to extract the information from Mr. Bishop."

All eyes turned to the bloody corpse tied to his office chair. Cade had avoided looking closely earlier, but now that he'd allowed himself a more than cursory glance, he couldn't look away.

Nathan Bishop's arms and legs were bound with thick rope to a heavy leather chair. His wounds were too numerous to take in all at once, but Cade immediately recognized them for what they were.

"Torture," he said softly, unaware he'd said it aloud until Alex appeared at his shoulder, nodding her concurrence.

"You're saying they broke into his house and tortured him?

How do you know it wasn't just some kids high on drugs?" Grisham moved closer to study the body. He tapped his pen on his scribbled notebook page. "Look at all these stab wounds. I've seen people go into a rage when they're high. Worked a case just last week where a man stabbed his wife thirty-nine times."

"They aren't stab wounds." Cade moved closer now, despite his good sense telling him otherwise. The victim's fingers were crushed, each bent in a different direction. Not from a single blow but as if they'd been deliberately "rearranged". His feet were blackened like they'd been held to a small fire. The cuts all over the body weren't made with a stabbing motion, but repeated slices in crisscross patterns all over the torso and limbs. Not deep enough to cause severe damage but enough that they would have caused excruciating pain. Cade had seen similar wounds on prisoners of war. What was different was the degradation of the skin around the wounds, as if the reverend had already begun to decay.

Two pairs of eyes studied him when he looked up— Grisham's with a wary admiration and Alex with approving curiosity. Though he'd been fine with her assessment of him previously and of all she seemed to infer about his war experiences, this wasn't a place he wanted her digging. Those particular memories of war remained a dark and scary place—a black hole with very little light shining through.

"So, three men break in and immediately bind Nathan Bishop in his chair and begin demanding information on the item they've been sent to steal," Alex recapped.

"They were sent by someone?" Grisham paused from writing

furiously in his notebook to frown in Alex's direction.

"Obviously." Which was *obviously* Alex's favorite word.

"It's not obvious to me," Cade spoke up. At least he could share Alex's verbal abuse with Grisham. The poor detective looked like he'd had almost enough of her for one day.

"The boot prints at the door indicate three men—two of them wearing muddy work boots, and another in industrial type boots. They're blue collar men. What would Nathan Bishop have they could possibly want? Not money, and it's unlikely they were here for confession. No, they were looking for secrets, which are the currency of the white collar set. But it was clearly something tangible since they walked around this room looking for it. They needed to bring *something* back to their employer."

"Wow," Cade breathed. "That was…"

"Let me guess, amazing?" A little of the zing was gone from Alex's tone as she finished his sentence.

Still he recoiled a little. "Sorry." Very unprofessional of him to act so in awe in front of Grisham… though from the detective's wide eyes and slightly agape mouth, it looked as though he echoed the sentiment.

"No, it's… fine." A slight crease formed between Alex's brows before she was on to something else. "The book, the Saint Augustine one, it has some significance. I avoided touching it so you could dust it for prints, but I think you'll find it's not a book at all. A safe of some sort, probably. Get that open and you'll know whether the intruders' methods were successful on Mr. Bishop. You can text me the answer to that."

"As soon as I know something, I'll let you know," Grisham

agreed with a wearied rub of his stubbly chin.

"Alex." Cade had barely been listening to the exchange between his roommate and the detective because something about the victim's clothing had caught his attention. Upon closer inspection, what had appeared to be a bloody cigar lying in the folds of Bishop's clothes proved to be something far more morbid. "There's a finger in his lap. Not his since all his seem to be intact… well, as intact as they can be after being crushed."

Alex and Grisham crowded around him to examine the severed finger.

"Index finger," Alex finally said. "The left one."

"I'll give you the index finger, but there's no way you can know it's the left one," Cade challenged. Not a thumb or a pinky, but that had been as far as he'd gotten with his analysis.

She responded with a sly smile. "He was probably wagging this finger at Bishop before he had it bitten off. When we find the owner of this finger, you'll see I'm right. He'll be a left handed man."

He wanted to say that "when" seemed very optimistic since they didn't have much to go on, but Alex had probably only given them the tip of the iceberg. While he'd thought she'd been wandering aimlessly around the room before Grisham's arrival, she'd managed to put together a convincing story of what happened to poor Nathan Bishop.

A commotion in the hallway sent them all backpedaling from the body. Grisham glanced at his watch, then to Alex.

"I'm afraid time's up. Are you collecting any souvenirs?"

Well, it certainly didn't work like this on TV. Weren't

detectives supposed to be fiercely protective of someone tampering with evidence before they'd had a chance to process it? What did Alex have on Grisham that he would let her run his crime scene?

"Just some dirt, I think." Alex reached inside her coat and produced several small paper envelopes and a pair of tweezers. Cade couldn't help but wonder what else she had in that coat.

"One minute," Grisham warned. "I'll stall Sarah." Then he stepped into the hallway where, Cade could see a sort of morbid circus of police, forensics, and ME personnel had gathered.

Alex crouched next to the body and held an envelope up to the section of rope binding Bishop's feet. With the precision of a surgeon, she scraped a miniscule amount of a dark, soil-like substance into the envelope and sealed it. She repeated the process with one of the several footprints near the study's main door.

"Had enough?" she asked him after she'd slid both envelopes into her pocket. There was that smile again—sly and charming and making it okay for him to embrace the flare of adrenaline and to say things like…

"Not even close."

CHAPTER FOUR

Of all the things Alex knew, how to work with a partner wasn't one of them. Not, of course, that she'd ever tried. Never felt the need to. People in general were much too boring to bother with. Besides, they got in the way of the work.

Cade, however, matched her stride for stride as they put distance between themselves and the crime scene. Normally, she would have retreated to her room with absolute silence for minutes that turned into hours to do nothing but think through possible theories for the crime.

It turned out that spouting off theories to her companion was much more fun. She hadn't expected to like his reactions so much, but there was something about the slight lift of his brows, the widening of his eyes, and the fall of his bottom lip when he breathed "…amazing" that gave her a rush. At least someone appreciated her brilliance, even if her deductions so far in this case had been elementary.

Three men, hired to obtain information from a clergyman at the cost of his life. What had they been searching for? Letters? Photos? Something not backed up electronically where it could be easily hacked. Maybe even something in code so the men wouldn't know what they'd found once they found it. It had likely been inside that book safe, which suggested they'd achieved their objective after all. If they'd failed to get the book open, they would have simply taken it with them. That it was put back on the shelf suggested—

"What are you going to do with those dirt samples?"

Oh. She'd forgotten Cade was there.

His brown eyes were full of questions though his fingers tapped incessantly against his leg as if his impatience was only barely contained. A soldier awaiting his orders. How fascinating, especially since he'd been quick to correct her that he was a combat medic and not, strictly speaking, a soldier. Obviously, it was a concession he'd made, but she'd need more data to determine the whole story.

She'd never had another person to experiment on, and as a result, rarely conducted social experiments. But he was really asking for it. Why else would he follow her without a clue where they were going? Judging by the slight flush in his cheeks, the straightness of his posture, he didn't mind not knowing. Interesting.

"Dirt from the rope and the intruders' shoes can tell us a lot about where they're from and the places they frequent." Discussing her theories and deductions aloud was something she'd occasionally done, but letting someone else tag along would likely minimize the stares she got when she did so.

So this experiment could be doubly beneficial.

"That was really incredible, what you did back there."

"That's not what most people say." Which was exactly why she found his reaction so amusing. In fact, she generally ignored anything uttered immediately after her deductions, but somehow Cade's simple "amazing"—she'd hoped he'd have a more extensive vocabulary—had pierced through the haze of information surrounding her brain.

"What do most people say?" He frowned slightly. Such a subtle gesture that he probably didn't know he was doing it. She'd already been cataloging his range of expressions. Frown number three meant there was an element of concern involved with his displeasure. But concern for what? His own safety? She wasn't dangerous per se, but she knew how she looked to most people. Especially after Sarah's typical tirade.

"It varies slightly, but there's usually a few expletives involved."

"Seriously?"

"Yes, well, when you deduce their cheating or addiction to drugs, people tend to be a bit less impressed." Come to think of it, why hadn't Cade been more upset with her initial impressions of him? His posture and frown number two indicated he didn't like talking about his military career, presumably because he didn't want people to know about his injuries. But she'd outed him in front of Tim, and he'd followed her home like a lost puppy.

"I'd say so," he replied as he slid his right hand into his coat pocket, his left still resting beside his left leg. "You know, not everything that's true needs to be spoken."

"Doesn't it? How boring." Was he still talking? Okay, maybe this was why she didn't work with a partner. He distracted her.

"You really don't care what you're supposed to do or say, do you?"

Now he was catching on. A little slower than she would have liked, but he'd gotten there all the same. "Sociopath, remember. I don't care how people are supposed to work. I just care about *the* work."

That silenced Cade for a while, but he didn't waver from his pace. Strange. This was usually the point where her admirers realized they'd get nothing in return and moved on. Then again, Cade Blackwell had fought a war and lived to tell—or *not* tell as he seemed to not want to talk—about it. Maybe he'd overlook a few things others didn't tolerate, but he'd eventually reach the same conclusion.

Alex was incapable of having friends. Expectation was a dangerous thing, and people's expectations for her seemed to involve the notion they could make her more human. As if that were somehow better than the way she was.

But being human didn't solve cases. It didn't provide answers. She only cared about emotion so much as it acted as a motive for her various cases. People committed heinous acts in the name of love, hate, and jealousy. Why would she want any part of that?

He'd handled the body well, though as a soldier he'd surely

seen his share. Still, she'd almost expected him to leave her high and dry at the crime scene.

She turned abruptly as they left the residential area behind, eyes focused on the dumpster along the side of a laundromat. Yes, this looked promising. Statistically this area was mostly likely.

"What are you doing?" Cade was on her heels again, nearly causing her to trip as she turned around to check the other side of the dumpster. His hands, good strong hands, clamped on her arms to right her, then he immediately turned her loose.

Alex brushed past him to examine the layers of dirt and grime covering the alley. Hard to tell—yes, there it was. Just like in Bishop's study, a size eleven men's work boot had left an impression in the damp grime. A few paces back, the prints disappeared as if the owner had climbed into a car and sped away. A pre-arranged meeting place then?

It really didn't matter. All she cared about was that at least one of the intruders had stopped by this dumpster.

"Open this." She indicated the heavy lid to Cade by tapping it with her hand. He obliged with a skeptical look in her direction. "Now give me a boost."

She was tall, and her heels gave her a couple extra inches, but she still couldn't see the entire dumpster. Hopefully she wouldn't actually have to climb in, but some sacrifices had to be made in the name of science.

"You're not doing what I think you're doing, are you?" Cade asked even as he cupped his hands to give her a leg up. He was curious, yes, and maybe a little doubtful, but not objectionable to her methods.

"Relax. It should be right on—oh there it is." Alex plucked the syringe from amidst a pile of lint trappings. Perfect. She squinted and noted the few droplets of liquid clinging to the inside of the syringe. Not much to work with, but if she was careful, it would be enough. All she had to do was—

With a wince and a groan, she found herself sitting on the ground in the alley. Oh. She'd forgotten he was the only thing holding her up. Why hadn't he lowered her when she turned? Then again, people seldom did what she thought they should.

Cade mirrored her position on the ground but not her nonchalance. Oh, that was a new frown. Number five. Anger with a hint of retribution. She wished she'd brought her notebook to catalog them.

"You have to talk to me," he ground out between clenched teeth. "Tell me when you want to move. Otherwise we both fall."

Of course he'd want communication. Cooperation. The army had hardwired him that way. Not really her strong suit, but possibly worth an effort if it would keep him around. He *had* been somewhat helpful so far, and the lure of a social experiment still excited her.

"Sorry. Next time I'll—"

"Next time? You think I'm going to follow you around and play your step stool while you pull hypodermic needles out of the garbage?"

Huh. That was different. Breathing deeply through flared nostrils, fingers curled into fists. He was nearly seething now.

Might as well finished him off. "Yes."

"I'm done," he spat as he pushed himself to a standing position and left her sitting in the filth.

This was why she didn't get involved with people. So exhausting to analyze why they were upset and what her response should be. But Cade appeared to be the exception and not the rule, and though his body language indicated he was mad, she'd seen the spark in his eyes when she'd rattled off the information at the crime scene.

"No, you're not." She stood and dusted the dirt from her coat as much as possible. "You're not done. In fact, you're just getting started. You like this."

He opened his mouth for a quick retort, then snapped it shut without saying anything. Hands on his hips, he studied the ground and shook his head. Perfect. He wasn't going to refute her statement.

"What normal person likes standing around a body and digging through trash for needles?" A little incredulous laugh punctuated his question.

"Who said anything about normal?"

His chin jerked up for his eyes to meet hers. She had him. The indicators had been there, but she'd avoided pressing his button until now. The uncomfortable tension between him and Tim, the way he stuck his shaking hand in his pocket, his forced manners...Cade was trying desperately to fit back into society and hating himself every time he couldn't. He wanted to be normal.

Perfectly acceptable parameters for an experiment. The

subject displays behavior outside the median. External stimuli may encourage movement along a bell curve, presumably either toward or away from the mean. Which stimuli would drive him further away from normal? What would the psychological effects of these variables be on the subject? Yes, that would work just fine.

Wait, where was he going? While she'd been devising the details of said experiment, Cade had apparently decided to leave. Without her. He stood at the mouth of the alley, back to her, as he glanced up and down the sidewalk.

"Where are you going?"

"To take a shower."

Alex knew the terseness of his words was designed to deter her from following. Perhaps even to make her think he'd written her off. But she knew better.

"I assume you're going back to the VA to do that since you don't have any clothes with you." Her words hit their mark, and his shoulders tensed. "In that case, do you mind picking up some milk on your way back to Stanton Park?"

He growled an unintelligible response as he spun on the ball of his foot and disappeared around the corner.

Excellent. He hadn't said no.

❧

Maybe this was what losing your mind felt like. Because as much as Cade's therapist assured him he wasn't crazy, he'd begun to suspect she was very wrong. If she knew he was considering returning to Stanton Park to get an update on a murder case from a self-proclaimed sociopath, Dr. Evanovich might be willing to concede this went a little beyond PTSD.

But that's exactly where he found himself. When he'd walked into his rooms at the VA to wash the alley filth off him, the sense of depression had almost overwhelmed him. Spartan furniture, no decorations, no personal items lying about… That room didn't hold a fraction of the warmth of Alex's—well, Mrs. Turner's—house. With the house's mismatched furnishings, he wouldn't have to be reminded of his lack of personal possessions. It seemed Alex and Mrs. Turner had already filled up the space.

He'd made up his mind. Moving in there only made sense. But, he thought as he sipped a black coffee on a bakery's outdoor patio and scanned the newspaper, he'd make Alex sweat about it. No point in running straight back to her when she seemed sure he'd do just that. And he wasn't buying milk either. If she wanted him there, she could buy the milk.

The news today looked like more of the same. He scanned the articles, noting that Representative Prince was apparently getting ready to push some controversial anti-terrorism legislation through. What else was new? Politicians always thought they knew best, especially when it came to playing with the lives of others.

Cade pulled his phone from his pocket and checked the time before resting it next to him on the table. 17:48. His military training had taught him to estimate time based on the position of the sun, but the tall buildings in downtown DC weren't exactly conducive to that. Most things in civilian life weren't compatible with what he'd learned in the army, but he'd known straight away about the wounds on Nathan Bishop's body. The army hadn't exactly trained him to recognize them, but it had been an unfortunate consequence of his time in the Middle East.

"Is this seat taken?"

Cade was about to say 'yes' when he peered just over the top of his paper, which he wasn't really reading any more, to see the owner of the soft, gentle voice.

A tall, willowy blond stood on the other side of his table, perfectly manicured hand on the back of the chair opposite him. Her hair was pulled into an equally perfect bun, which somehow directed all the attention to her pale blue eyes. She raised one dark blond brow as a reminder of the question she'd just asked.

"Oh, right, sorry." Cade sat the paper on the table and gestured for her to join him. He snuck a quick glance around the patio, or what he could see of it due to his horrible peripheral vision on the right side—Alex had been right about that as well. The bakery was busy, but an empty table or two still remained, which meant this woman had *chosen* to sit with him.

Why? He wasn't vain enough to assume she found him attractive, though it wasn't outside the realm of possibility. She was stunning in her own right, so something felt a little odd about her singling him out. But who was he to argue with such beautiful company? He couldn't recall the last time he'd had a date.

"Enjoying your coffee?" she asked as she sipped her own drink and leaned back in her chair. There was a sort of restrained grace in the way she moved.

He didn't understand why, but a faint warning registered in his gut. Something was... off. "Yeah, I guess so."

Better to remain casual until he figured it out. And he was

probably overreacting. It's not like Al-Qaeda was going to jump out from behind that potted plant.

Her eyes flicked over him, giving him the distinct impression of tigress stalking her prey. In the span of a second, he'd managed to lose control of this situation.

"You're confused." A simple statement, but all the gentleness she'd affected moments before seeped from her voice, replaced by cool steeliness.

"I'm sorry. Do I know you?" His head injury *had* caused some memory loss, but it had been temporary. Or so he thought. Because he was pretty sure he would've remembered meeting this woman, but it was the only explanation for the strange sense of familiarity she oozed.

"Not exactly." She raised her cup to her red lips and took a sip, leaving an impression in lipstick on the paper cup. Even that seemed like a calculated move. She wasted movement even less than words. "But I know you quite well."

Careful not to react, Cade pressed his lips together and waited on her to continue.

"Captain Cade Blackwell, combat medic from the Third Battalion of the 75th Ranger Regiment. Recently retired due to an IED explosion which left you unable to fulfil your duty."

"I fulfilled my duty." His jaw burned with tension as he clenched his teeth around each word. The faint warning now echoed loudly as his muscles tightened to full alert. He should really walk away, but the same curiosity that drew him to Alex demanded he remain seated.

"That duty, certainly. But you're not finished, are you? Still a soldier, am I right? You're just looking for a different war."

"Who are you?" He didn't correct her like he had Alex. What was the use when she already knew too many details?

"Is this trick not as fun when someone besides Alex Holst is doing it?" The woman studied her nails before leveling a stare at Cade. "Don't look so surprised. She's hardly the only game in town."

Information. He had to pry some sort of information from this woman. She knew Alex, but from the way she spoke her name, the relationship appeared to be antagonistic at best. Had Alex gotten herself into some sort of trouble?

"It's a nice trick," he said slowly, trying to buy himself some time to think.

"Not the only one I know. Would you like to see my vanishing act? I could make you disappear from this patio, and not even Alex would know where to find you."

He resisted the urge to tell her he'd like to see her try because there was an iciness to her voice that suggested she wasn't lying. Who was this woman, and why was she talking to him?

Calm, slow breaths filtered in and out of his nose. Control. He needed to regain control. Pretense had no place here. "It's going to take a lot more than that to scare me. Army Ranger, remember?"

"Hooah," she muttered flippantly. "It's not my intent to scare you, Captain, just question you. What is your connection to Alex Holst?"

Alex. This *was* all about Alex. It figured. First the smugglers, then the murder, now an interrogation. Life certainly wasn't boring, but this felt…different.

"I've known her…" he glanced at his phone again, "just over twenty-four hours." Had it really only been a day? "I wouldn't say that's enough for a connection."

"You're moving in with her."

He swallowed hard. He'd been willing to concede this woman could have Googled him to find out about his military career, but how could she possibly know about the house in Stanton Park? "I think it's none of your business."

"And you were at a crime scene with her today."

A soft beep from his phone indicated an incoming text, and he looked away from the woman long enough to read it.

Don't forget the milk.

Alex really did have impeccable timing. Also, he wasn't buying the milk, and how did she get his phone number?

"What do you want from me?" The text from Alex had relaxed him marginally, and he crossed his arms and leaned back in his chair to make sure his companion knew it.

"Alex doesn't have friends. You'd be better off to walk away now."

"Why? Because she's a sociopath?" Rude, somewhat cold, assuming. Yes, she was all those things, but none of them had been enough to deter him.

"For starters, yes." Her eyes drifted down to where his hands rested on table. On instinct, he started to hide them below the table, but she shook her head. "Let me see your hand."

He didn't have to ask which one she meant. Against all

reason, he held out a steady right hand to her. She didn't touch, but leaned in slightly to study it. To the left of his hand, his phone beeped again.

Stanton Park. Now.

His heart thumped against his chest. Was Alex in some sort of trouble? Surely she'd call the police if there were an emergency.

"Interesting."

He'd almost forgotten the woman was studying his hand. "What is?"

"Your tremor isn't brought on by your post-traumatic stress, though you obviously still bear some of the hallmarks. But your hand… I've threatened you, set you on edge, and you're steady as a rock. Either you're stupid—in which case Alex would have disposed of you already—or fear has the opposite effect on you. It wakes you up."

"I'm not afraid of you."

"So stupid then." She reclined back in her chair and shrugged. "Of course, I might have surmised that from your willingness to move in with Alex after having known her for… what was it again? Twenty-four hours? Are you attracted to her?"

"I'm not answering that." Meaning, of course, that he *had* just answered.

"No need to," she confirmed. Her stillness unnerved him. Most people fidgeted or tapped their fingers—something. Only her lips and eyes moved when she spoke. "Still, I don't imagine she's encouraged any sort of affection. Relationships aren't really her area. You'd be better off to stay away from her."

"I'm confused as to why you think this is any of your business."

"I make it my business to know things." Her chin tilted up slightly as her lips pursed. "And I'm very good at what I do."

"So am I." The thinly veiled threat had little visible effect on his companion.

"You're not rich."

Cade laughed at the non-sequitur. "Are you concerned about my ability to pay the rent?"

"I haven't dealt in anything as common as money in years. Secrets are the new currency, Captain Blackwell. But for a man like you, I'd be willing to pay for a few secrets. Not about you, of course. I can read all yours I care to know. But some information on Ms. Holst could prove very valuable to you."

Ah. There it was. "Not interested."

"I haven't told you how much."

"If you know Alex, you know she won't tell me anything about her personal life. I'm not even sure she has a personal life."

"Of course she doesn't." A spark of something flared in her pale eyes. "I'd just like to know what she's up to. She does tend to get herself into trouble."

That was definitely true. Apparently associating with Alex was enough to get him interrogated by this woman.

Abruptly, the woman stood and grabbed her cup. "I've enjoyed our chat, Captain Blackwell." She nodded once toward him, then started to walk away. Three steps from the table she paused and looked at him over her shoulder. "You're too noble for your own good. A bit of a character flaw in this case. If you know what's good for you, you'll stay away from Alex Holst."

When he blinked, she'd already disappeared into the small crowd. For a long moment, he couldn't move as the incredulity of the events washed over him. This wasn't his life. This kind of stuff just didn't happen to him. He wasn't sure it happened to anybody except in movies.

He reached for his phone, intending to respond to Alex's text, but stopped when he saw his right hand poised in midair over the phone. Not a trace of a tremor. A wry smile worked its way to his lips. Maybe his mystery woman was right. The adrenaline rush he usually associated with battle was just beginning to ebb from this encounter.

Only one way to test this theory. If staying away from Alex was the safest thing to do, his only recourse was to get back to Stanton Park as quickly as possible.

CHAPTER FIVE

By the time he returned to the house in Stanton Park and Mrs. Turner giddily handed him a key—did everyone assume he was moving in?—the faint ghost of a tremor had returned to his fingers. Barely enough to be noticeable to the naked eye, but he could feel it all the same, and his heart sank. It wasn't gone for good. He needed that rush to still it. Just like a junky looking for his next hit.

That was confirmed when he took the stairs two at a time and emerged into the living room. Though he was far from familiar with the house, the stillness of the room struck him as strange, made him uneasy. He didn't have to wonder long what had set him on edge. Hand still resting on the stair railing, he swiveled his head until his eyes found her.

His heart leapt into his throat as he quickly scanned the room, then darted toward her. Alex sat in a chair in the center of the room, ropes wound around her body, holding her upright. With her head bowed, her dark hair obscured her face, and her stillness made him question if she was still breathing.

"Don't touch me," she snapped without looking up though he still stood several feet from her.

He exhaled in relief and immediately took a step back. Definitely breathing then.

"Who did this to you?" His thoughts immediately went to the woman at the bakery. Had she only been sent to distract him while someone else came after Alex? But Mrs. Turner hadn't acted like she'd heard a thing.

"I did, of course." Her voice sounded tight, uncomfortable, as she raised her head to look him over. Pale eyes danced over his features.

"Of course." Because she was crazy.

"Did you get the milk?"

He laughed, paced away from her, and roughed a hand over his face. Unbelievable.

"What?" she demanded, clearly perturbed to not be let in on the joke. "Why wouldn't you get the milk? I even texted to remind you. That's what roommates do, right?"

That gave him pause. She was trying, in her own weird way, to act like a normal roommate. He was pretty sure that ship had sailed. Somehow, the bondage negated the effort.

"Let me untie you." It seemed impossible she could've bound herself up like this, feet strapped together, a rope across her abdomen and collar bones, and her hands bound tightly in her lap. Too tightly. Her fingers trembled, and her skin looked paler than usual.

"Fine," she consented with a huff and a toss of her hair over her shoulder. "Not a very useful experiment anyway."

She paused, and he looked up from where he'd knelt to untie her feet. With that proximity, he saw streaks of amber in her gray-green eyes. More layers, more intrigue. Nothing was as it initially seemed with Alex.

"But maybe you could try to tie me up while I fight back. I need to see if it's possible that all three men were involved in tying Bishop up or if one would've sufficed."

"We're not doing that." The knots around her feet finally gave way, and he started on her hands. His fingers worked of their own accord as he untangled the rope. "Besides, I could tie you down with one hand, so it's hardly a good experiment."

When she didn't immediately respond, he looked up to find her eyebrows raised and an appreciative smirk on her lips. "That's… good to know."

"How did you text me if you were tied up?"

"I sent those right before I tied myself up." She wiggled against the ropes and inhaled a painful sounding breath. "Knew you'd be home soon."

He smiled a little at her choice of words. Home. "You missed me." He couldn't resist a little teasing, especially when she was still strapped to the chair.

"I think better aloud. It's nice to have someone to listen."

It might have been the first normal thing he'd heard her say so he let it pass without comment. With her hands freed, he moved behind her to work on the knot connecting the rope at her stomach and shoulders. "Do I even want to know how you managed this?"

"Certain skills are required in the field of criminal investigation. This is just the tip of the iceberg. I also—" Her diatribe cut off in a near yelp as he tugged on the rope, effectively cutting off her air.

"Oops." Of course he'd done it entirely on purpose. Brilliant as she was, someone needed to stop her from showing off all the time. He let her go just as quickly though, and she was on her feet in a flash, shaking out her limbs and pulling her hair into a messy bun at the nape of her neck.

"Now, on to more important things." She rushed around the room like a whirlwind, scattering papers, rearranging envelopes, until she found her phone.

"I've been busy while you've been away… *not* buying the milk." She muttered the latter, but not softly enough. "I've analyzed the soil samples from the rope and the footprints at Bishop's murder."

"How did you analyze them?" Her eyes flicked toward the kitchen, and he stepped around her to look. Spread across the small table was a microscope and a myriad of glass bottles containing questionable looking liquids. "You turned our kitchen into a chemistry lab?"

"In the name of science, Cade." She stood shoulder to shoulder with him, both staring at the mess on the table. "Don't you want to catch Bishop's killers?"

He chanced a look in her direction and studied her profile in the brief instant before she turned to look right back. "So a few drops of acid on the dirt and you know who the killer is?"

"Killer*s*." She accentuated the plural. "And don't be ridiculous. It's really a complex analysis. I have a paper on it around here somewhere. First I had to—"

"Alex, I really don't care. Can we just cut to the part where you tell me what the next step is?

An exasperated huff parted her lips. "Fine. But you're missing almost everything important."

"Good thing I have a genius in front of me to distill it down then."

"Basically, the soil samples from the rope and footprints had a certain consistency, which led me to believe they came from either the river area or a pit because they retained large amounts of moisture, and it hasn't rained in more than a week. Upon further analysis, I was able to compare the samples and the traces of pollen they contained to my catalog and determine it came from soil north of the Potomac, though not along the bank because the nitrogen…okay, fine. I'll skip that part. Probably from some sort of pit then. That narrows down the area to some sort of construction or digging zone."

"I'm not sure that *does* narrow it down." He could name half a dozen construction sites north of the river, but it wouldn't get them any closer to the killers.

"Well, see, this is where Grisham was actually helpful for once. Besides confirming that the book safe was empty, which I already knew, he sent me this." She held up her phone to show him a zoomed in shot of something shiny in a pool of crimson. Blood definitely. "Photos of the crime scene. From these, I was able to see something we all missed because it was under the body. A scalpel." Her smirk turned into a wide smile, clearly pleased with herself.

"That could have been used to make those cuts on his torso."

"Exactly." She slid her phone back in her pocket. "And what's even better is that there was a small inscription blade. GUH."

It took a moment for those initials to register. "Georgetown University Hospital. The murder weapon was from the hospital?"

"Not the murder weapon, but I'm getting to that. But yes, the scalpel used to torture our victim came from the hospital. I can even tell you which department."

"Well, surgery's the obvious choice, but that's not right," he began slowly, ignoring the way her eyes widened at his attempted reasoning. "They would probably have disposable sterile scalpels so they don't run the risk of infection, and they wouldn't need their initials on a blade they're going to throw away anyway."

"Sound reasoning," Alex concurred, with a note of surprise lurking underneath. "Go on."

"Well, so the blade has to be from somewhere they reuse blades… somewhere it doesn't matter."

"Perfect, yes. Now where?" she prompted, leaning closer with sharp, clear eyes.

"The morgue?"

"My conclusion as well. So, should we pay a visit to the morgue?" She spun on her heels and pulled her coat from the couch. Just as she was about to put it on, her phone buzzed and she frowned at it. "Oh, never mind. Oliver says he's gone home for the day."

"Who's Oliver?"

"Pathology resident who sometimes does me a favor or two. Visitors aren't allowed in the morgue, strictly speaking, but we have an understanding."

"Of course you do." He shoved his hands in his pockets, and the key Mrs. Turner had given him brushed his fingers. "So, I guess I'm moving in…"

"I gathered that from the duffle bag you dropped at the top of the stairs."

In his rush to check on Alex, he'd forgotten he even carried his clothes in. It wasn't everything from his room at the VA, but a few articles of clothing, his laptop, and his gun would suffice for a night or two. Long enough for him to test out this arrangement. The gun had been an afterthought, but as he'd turned to leave his apartment, the mystery woman's words replayed in his head. A threat or a warning, he wasn't sure. Still too early to tell which of these women was the dangerous one. Either way, he'd feel safer with his weapon.

"So do you want to make a trip to the grocery store tonight?" He was careful in his word choice this time, lest he be accused of asking her out again. "I'm starving and there's nothing to eat here."

"I'm not hungry," she replied absently, absorbed in something on her phone. "Don't forget the milk this time, though."

"Buy your own milk. I'm ordering pizza." He retrieved his bag from the landing by the stairs without a glance in her direction.

An inexplicable grin pulled at the corner of his mouth as he trotted up the other set of stairs to claim his bedroom. No pretenses, no pretending to be polite. This had the potential to be the best decision he'd made in a long time.

Cade bolted upright in bed, disoriented and coughing as he tried to inhale. Instead of crisp air, his lungs filled with the taste of smoke. It took too long to convince himself that he *had* woken up from his dream, and he wasn't still in Afghanistan with a bomb exploding right in front of him, setting his world ablaze.

The smoke was definitely real, though. No amount of blinking his tired eyes or a reality check could clear it from his lungs. What if the house was on fire? Mrs. Turner, Alex, were they still inside? He pulled a shirt over his head, shoved his feet in his tennis shoes, and yanked the door open. The door to Alex's bedroom stood wide open, but he couldn't make out any sign of her in the dark. From the bottom on the stairs, light seeped up, dulled by the tendrils of smoke curling to the second floor.

He raced down the stairs, skipping the last three and landing lightly on his feet in the living room. The source of the smoke became immediately apparent as Alex sat on the couch, watching the curtains smolder with orange embers.

Every nasty thing he wanted to yell in her general direction got stopped up in his throat with another inhale of the smoke. Through another coughing fit, he stormed across the room and ripped the curtains from the walls. The rod and hardware fell with a crash around him as he proceeded to stomp out every glowing flame on the dusty fabric.

Satisfied the immediate danger had passed, he drug his gaze from the curtains up to Alex, who watched him keenly from her spot on the couch. Nothing was said for several moments as they surveyed each other. Once again, so many angry words went through his mind without exiting his mouth. He chanced a glance at his hand. Perfectly still.

Alex watched him all the way across the room until he sank into "his" chair, slightly out of breath both from the smoke and the excitement. Then, she stood and moved to take the chair opposite him.

"You okay?" Not the first question that popped into his head, but maybe the time for asking *why* Alex did things had passed.

"Of course." She peered at him over the rim of her coffee cup. "It was just an experiment. I had it all under control."

"Is that why everything was on fire?"

"It was hardly everything. Just the curtains."

He paused. He'd just put out a fire in their home. Now he faced a crossroads. Lecture Alex for her insanity, or embrace it. "I didn't like those curtains anyway."

Alex sputtered as she nearly spit coffee everywhere. Her face split into a wide grin as she recovered. A hint of pride sparkled in her eyes as she let out a short, disbelieving laugh. "Took you long enough to get down here. I thought I'd need to set fire to the tablecloth next."

"I was asleep. You know, sleep…the thing most people do at four o'clock in the morning." When all else failed, he relied on sarcasm. Anger was wasted on Alex, and he didn't for one minute think he could order her to do anything.

"Most people are boring." She took another careful sip of her coffee. "And you were having a nightmare."

That sucked the levity out of the room as he became her sole focus once again. "How did you know?"

"Your PTSD is quite real. Nightmares are a common side effect." She didn't offer more details, and he didn't ask for any. "What do you dream about?"

A sarcastic "can't you figure it out?" was on his tongue, but he changed his mind. She probably could figure it out, but she'd asked instead. That meant something.

"The IED explosion." He cleared his throat. "I was leading a MEDEVAC, and I bent over to tie my shoe and everything went white. Sometimes it ends there, other times it's about the attack immediately after."

He wasn't sure what he expected her response to be. Maybe a look of boredom, some psychoanalysis, but not the curious tilt of her head or the knowing purse of her lips.

"That's why you never untie your shoes." Her voice was uncharacteristically soft, with a gentleness he hadn't known she was capable of. Perhaps she didn't know either.

"That's why." He didn't bother to ask how she knew. She'd seen him in two pairs of tennis shoes so far, both double knotted but loose enough for him to slip his feet in and out. Just as he'd done before he raced down from his bedroom.

She didn't speak again for some time. Cade raided the refrigerator to pull out the last two slices of pizza and inhaled them cold while sitting opposite her.

With her knees hugged to her chest and eyes closed, he took the opportunity to study her. In her blue flannel pants and loose fitting gray t-shirt, she could easily pass for a college student pulling an all-nighter. Except he knew she'd been awake round the clock for something far more serious than a biochem exam. Still, she looked young, though not necessarily vulnerable.

Even with her keen eyes closed and sharp tongue silenced, she gave off an icy air. Probably no one had ever said she was friendly or warm. Not that those adjectives were everything. He'd tried to be both those things when reconnecting with his old friends after the war only to find it was difficult to fit a square peg in a round hole. War had whittled him down to sharp edges, though probably not as sharp as Alex.

In her case, it didn't really matter. Anyone who spent five seconds with her could see how brilliant she was. God had certainly gifted her in that respect. What she lacked in manners, she made up for in intellect. She was one of a kind.

Or was she?

Maybe he should ask Alex about the woman who'd cornered him at the bakery. She'd seemed to know Alex, maybe better than he wanted to admit, so it wasn't unreasonable to think Alex knew her as well.

"So, something weird happened when I was on my way back here last night," he began.

"Stop talking." Alex's eyes remained closed as she readjusted her posture so her long legs draped over the arm of the chair. "I need to think, and you're distracting me."

"You said you liked to think aloud."

"Shh, not now."

So much for the progress he thought they'd made.

"I'm going back to bed then." Back to back nights of nightmares and being awoken to a ceremonial curtain burning were catching up with him. So much for hardly even noticing Alex was here.

He awoke for the second time that morning—yes, still morning as the clock now read 9:28—to the blankets being yanked from him and his bedroom light flicked on without warning.

"Up," Alex insisted as she stalked around the room. She was fully dressed in what seemed to be her typical attire—dark trousers, a crisp button-up, and her coat hanging over her arm. "We're going to the morgue."

Telling her no and going back to sleep crossed his mind, but then he remembered the stolen scalpel and decided against it. Four uninterrupted hours of sleep ought to be enough to get by on for a while.

"Did you get any sleep?" he mumbled as he sat up and rubbed his eyes.

"Can't sleep. A man tortured for information, hired killers, a stolen scalpel. It's like Christmas."

"Not good," he groaned as he fell back on the bed and pulled a pillow over his head. "You can't say that in public."

It was amazing she hadn't been arrested for comments like that already. Not that he actually believed she was capable of murder, but it did give a little weight to the warning he'd received at the bakery.

"It's not public. Just you. Now get up and get dressed. I'm leaving in ten minutes." She breezed out of his room leaving her usual wake of snark and confusion.

Eight minutes later, he met her at the foot of the stairs with his hair still wet and his shirt clinging to his damp skin. He'd learned to get ready at a moment's notice in the army, so ten minutes felt like a luxury.

"Good." Alex checked her watch then nodded. "Let's walk and I'll catch you up on everything you missed last night."

He guessed that was best case scenario for both of them. He'd gotten his sleep, and she'd been able to think in silence. Now she'd have a chance to talk it out, just like she'd told him she liked as he untied her from the chair.

Whatever. It worked, so he wouldn't question it for now.

CHAPTER SIX

Cade led the way out the front door and down the stairs to the sidewalk outside their home—the first time he'd ever used the proper entrance instead of Mrs. Turner's apartment—and turned right to head toward the Metro. He'd barely taken two steps when he was hauled backward by a surprisingly strong grip on his arm.

"Not that way," Alex informed him.

"Well, I'm not walking all the way to Georgetown." The air was brisk and cold, and he put his hands in his pockets and ducked a little further into his jacket.

"We're taking a cab."

With the sort of perfect timing that no real person could predict, a cab pulled up to the curb in front of them. Cade simply shook his head as he climbed in the car behind her. He closed the door as Alex gave the driver their destination, then fixed her eyes on something outside her window.

"What have you got against the Metro?"

"People," she muttered without turning around.

He couldn't argue with her there.

"So are you going to fill me in?"

"Oh right," she said after a moment, as if she'd forgotten he was even there. "You were quite observant with those wounds yesterday. Do you remember what was unusual about them?"

"A reverend was sliced and diced with his fingers broken and an extra finger in his lap. I hope it's all unusual." But for her, it probably wasn't.

"You're religious, aren't you?" It was starting to irritate him that she refused to look at him. "You're insistent about referring to him as a reverend, and I found a rather well-worn Bible in your duffle bag."

"Because he *was* a reverend, and this is not about me." He paused his rant to consider what she'd inadvertently implied. It wasn't even worth it to comment on her searching his bag. "Besides, war has a funny way of getting your priorities in order."

"All that death and violence, your injury, and you still choose to believe in God." She continued to look out the window as if she hadn't just hit at the core of him. As if she wasn't slicing him as neatly as that scalpel but with her words instead.

"There are no atheists in the trenches." Not a trace of humor remained in his tone. If anything, he was more certain than ever. It was difficult to tell with Alex if her opinions were the opposite of his, or if she was just making the argument for the sake of argument. This, however, was important enough for him to ask her straight out. "Are you not religious?"

"No time for theology discussions." She finally shifted to face him, tucking her right leg under her. Her face was blank. Nothing to go on to decide if her change of topic was an evasion or just because she was bored. The woman had set fire to their curtains in the name of an experiment only that morning. That she would probe a subject and then change it just for the heck of it wasn't outside the realm of possibility.

"You started it," he couldn't resist pointing out.

"And now I've finished it. So Bishop's body…think about the skin around the cuts. What do you remember?"

Though he really wanted to probe further into the religion issue, it was pointless. It was a touchy subject even for normal people, and Alex certainly wasn't that. "It was degraded, breaking down. Seemed a bit premature considering he'd been dead for less than twelve hours."

Alex raised her brows but ducked her chin to look at him in a way that could only be described as impressed. "Good. I wasn't sure you'd noticed."

"I'm not blind, and I did have a couple years of medical school."

"Fascinating." She rubbed her lip and narrowed her eyes as if she could read more into his history. "You didn't finish. Why? You're not the type to leave something half done."

"September 11th happened." Though no one else had understood, Cade hadn't agonized over the decision. The devastating attack demanded a response, one he wanted to be part of sooner rather than later. Medical school could wait. He'd wanted to serve his country in any way he could when it needed him most.

"You had the schooling for an officer and the interest in medicine, so you became a combat medic. Why didn't you ever go back and finish medical school?"

"I've spent eight of the last ten years in a warzone," he admitted. "That doesn't leave much time for school. I knew enough to do what I needed to do. Also enough to know a man shouldn't be decomposing while he's still in rigor mortis."

"Excellent. There was also an injection site in Bishop's neck, which was nearly invisible due to the dried blood."

"But you saw it of course."

"Of course," she echoed. "Now, put it all together. A man tortured for information, needle mark on his neck, an extra finger in his lap, bits of blood and tissue in his teeth. What does that equal?"

He had no idea. "A psychopath?"

Alex sighed heavily. "You people keep using that word, but it doesn't mean what you think it means."

"Did you just make a Princess Bride reference?"

Her brows knit in a confused frown. "I don't think there were any royal weddings involved."

Cade chuckled softly. How could someone so brilliant be so clueless? "It's a movie."

"A man is dead. Try to stay on topic. Now, the needle mark obviously suggests something was injected, but what? The state of his skin indicates a volatile substance, and the finger in his lap—which he clearly bit off one of his attackers—tells us it induces a state of madness, maybe even hallucinations."

God help him, there was something attractive in the way she did that. Just random, unusual clues she managed to put together to tell a story, which—if her relationship with the police was any indication—was usually proven true in the end. "That's how you knew to look for the needle in the trash."

"Three men hired by someone else do carry out this kind of robbery aren't leaving a getaway car sitting out front. They knew they'd be in the building a while and in a part of town where most people don't park on the street. The car would certainly be noticed. So it stands to reason they walked to the house. Couldn't have been far, though, because they were still tracking mud from near Georgetown on their boots when they got inside. Therefore, someone either let them out, or they had a car parked a couple streets away.

"The route we followed when we left the crime scene was the most obvious path for them to take as they fled. And they would have taken the obvious one because they're not criminal masterminds, just hired hands. There was no syringe present in Bishop's study, and we know they didn't enter the other parts of the house because of the locked doors. Therefore, they had to dispose of the syringe somewhere. In an adrenaline rush, their first instinct would be to simply get away. By the time one of them realized he was still holding the syringe, they were likely almost to their car. I simply looked for the most obvious dumpster along the getaway route. In the dirt around the trash, I found several boot prints consistent with those at the crime scene."

The words hit him like a gale force wind—fast and furious and enough to knock him over if he wasn't already sitting down. "Wow," he breathed through his agape mouth. "How does your brain work that fast? You didn't say a word, and you already had it worked out before we left the scene."

"I couldn't say a word or Grisham would have expressly forbid me from taking the syringe." There was that sly smile again. "But he can hardly say I stole evidence since the dumpster isn't part of the crime scene."

"You have a loop hole for everything, don't you?"

"Wide enough to drive a truck through. Ah, we're here." Alex threw some bills at the driver and gracefully leaped from the cab parked on the curb of a rather nondescript building he supposed was the back side of the hospital. Definitely not the door they'd exited two days before.

Had it only been two days?

"What did you do with the syringe, then?" She'd explained the dirt and her narrowing down of the location, but he didn't believe she'd sit on a piece of evidence like that syringe.

"I came straight here after you left me yesterday and borrowed a mass spectrometer."

"When you say borrowed…"

"Doesn't matter." She waved him off with one hand as the other furiously typed something into her phone. "I just wish I had known about the scalpel while I was here, and we'd be at least twelve hours ahead of where we are now."

And he would've gotten zero sleep instead of the precious few hours he'd grabbed. Thank God for the little things.

"So if these guys stole a scalpel from the morgue most likely, and had access to some sort of poison or drug, maybe they worked here?" It seemed to be the most logical explanation. Maybe they should start in human resources with a list of employees and work from there. Though he had to admit that sounded incredibly boring.

"One of them worked here." Alex paced a small stretch of the sidewalk and glanced again at her phone. "They all have menial jobs, very low paying. Desperate for money, which is why they agreed to kill a man for a reason they probably didn't understand."

"But why would whoever hired them need three people?" It seemed a little excessive for attacking a peaceful clergyman. Even without his special training, Cade wouldn't have needed any help to subdue the reverend.

Alex paused, gasped softly, and then whirled on Cade, her coat flapping out behind her like a cape. "That's clever. He hired a specialist."

Though she looked right at him, the glaze in her pale eyes suggested it wasn't Cade she saw at all.

"A specialist?"

"Yes." She shook her head, and this time looked directly into his eyes. "You're absolutely right. Three men is too many. It's reckless. They might talk, they're more likely to be seen in a group like that... Why hire three? Unless one of them had a special skill. Yes. One of them is the muscle, one the expert in prolonging torture, and the other has access to or knows how to make a poison that makes the victim go mad before it kills him."

"But why?" Her theory made sense, as always, but why choose a poison when they could have just as easily slit the man's throat?

Her brow furrowed until a little wrinkle formed between her eyes. "I don't know yet. But if Oliver will let us in, we'll be one step closer to finding out."

Not even a minute later, a man in a white coat opened the door with a sheepish look on his slightly scruffy face. "Sorry, I had to wash my hand and degown. I was in the middle of weighing organs."

"About time," Alex muttered as she breezed past him, leaving Cade to stand awkwardly in front of the young man.

Oliver—it wasn't a great leap to assume this was the man Alex had mentioned—took in Cade's figure with slightly widened eyes that made Cade straighten his spine another inch or two. He was still in decent shape, still intimidating, but Oliver looked at him like the nerdy kid in movies always looked at the popular kids. Awe and a little envy.

"I'm with her," Cade finally said since it didn't appear Oliver was going to offer to break the ice.

"With Alex?" Oliver asked as he adjusted his dark rimmed glasses. "But I-she usually doesn't... She doesn't bring people with her."

Did he detect a bit of jealousy, or was it just surprise that made Oliver's voice hitch slightly at the end? It's not like Cade had any answers for the man. For whatever reason, Alex had deemed him worthy to tag along, at least for the moment, and the reactions of everyone they'd come in contact with suggested it was outside her norm.

"Cade," Alex's voice echoed down the short hallway Oliver still blocked with his wiry frame, "we don't have all day."

With an apologetic nod, Cade stepped around the smaller man and entered the sterile hallway. Beige tile, white walls, and fluorescent lights welcomed him.

"This way," Oliver mumbled as he shut the door and moved down the hallway. "She'll be in the lab."

Lab was actually a very loose term for the room Alex had appropriated. Once Cade and Oliver stepped inside, the tiny room felt like a small closet, not unlike the one where Tim had stitched Alex up that first day. This space, however, was outfitted with two small tables—both covered with microscopes, test tube racks, and several unlabeled bottles that looked conspicuously like those she'd laid out on their kitchen table. Alex stood over one of two large machines which took up nearly all of two walls.

"Can I help?" Oliver asked, a little too eagerly, as he pushed his glasses higher on his face.

Alex, her eyes fixed on a computer attached to one of the machines, completely ignored him. His enthusiastic smile fell as Cade watched his hope crumble. Poor guy. He clearly worshipped her, and she wouldn't even give him the time of day unless she needed into the lab or morgue.

"Could you get us a list of people who have access to the morgue?" If Alex wasn't going to utilize Oliver, then Cade would. Make him feel useful. Besides, that information would be necessary to narrow down who could have taken the scalpel.

"I…" Oliver straightened as confusion flicked across his face. Cade could see him trying to work out who exactly he was, and what gave him the authority to speak on Alex's behalf. Oliver's eyes flicked to Alex, as if he expected her to put Cade in his place. "I can give you a list, sure, but I might be able to help more if I knew what you were looking for."

"A janitor, perhaps," Alex spoke up, though she didn't look at them. "Maybe an assistant. Who is in charge of cleaning the instruments after an autopsy?"

"It depends on the day. If there's an assistant on duty, they'll clean them. If not, the pathologist will just put them in to soak. Some of the guys in housekeeping will clean them when they come in, but most won't touch them."

Alex turned her head slightly in their direction. "Names?"

"Um, Scott, I think…for one of them anyway." Oliver wrinkled his nose as he tried to remember the information Alex required. "He's pretty cool. Reminds me of my grandfather—"

"That's not him," she interrupted, leaving the machine behind and busying herself searching for something in the mess she'd left on the table. "He won't be old enough to be anyone's grandfather unless he started very young. More likely in his thirties or forties."

"Oh. Well that would be Mason, then." Oliver shifted his weight as if something made him uncomfortable.

"You don't like him." So Alex had noticed, too. Everything else forgotten, she turned her sharp eyes on Oliver, who ducked his head and looked at his shoes.

"I don't see him much," Oliver said to the floor. "He's

mostly here at night, so I'm usually gone by then. But he's kinda odd. I think he used to be in the army because he's got all these military tattoos."

Cade thought of his own bare arms and the dozens of posers he'd seen with military tattoos, but didn't correct Oliver. Alex had said one of the men was likely an expert in prolonging torture. It wasn't the sort of thing the military taught, but depending on where Mason was stationed, it was entirely likely he could have picked up some creative interrogation skills.

"Doesn't say much, but he gives me this look sometimes…" Oliver punctuated his words with a slight shudder. "He's never done anything as far as I know, but if he comes in when Molly's down here, she'll usually call me so she won't have to be alone with him."

That had to be their guy. Cade looked to Alex for confirmation and got it in the form of a gleam in her eyes.

"Is he left handed?" She tensed, looking like she might pounce on her prey at any moment.

Oliver blinked in surprise. "I don't know? I mean, I've only seen the guy mopping so it's not like I could tell."

"Of course you could." Alex threw her hands up and stomped around the table to stand in front of Cade and Oliver. "Statistically speaking, a person will place their dominant hand near the end of the mop and grip the handle further down with their opposite hand."

"I hope you plan on experimenting with the mopping," Cade quipped before he could remind himself this was hardly the time to be the nagging roommate.

The corner of her mouth quirked up slightly. "It doesn't matter right now. Mason works night shift, right? Does he have a locker, a coat, anything personal he keeps around here?"

"Sure. We let them hang their coats inside the morgue so no one will bother them, and they won't have to go all the way upstairs to their lockers if they want to go outside for a smoke break or something."

"Then we need to see it." Alex brushed past them and exited the tiny room. "Well, c'mon. We need to be let into the morgue."

The authoritative edge to Alex's tone had Oliver snapping to attention, and it took an effort on Cade's part not to follow suit. Though he'd been an officer, he was used to jumping at those sorts of orders.

They passed no one as Oliver led them from the makeshift lab to the doors at the end of the hallway where he had to use his badge to enter. Even though he'd known what to expect, a small chill still shuddered Cade's spine when the cooler air hit his skin. From his position just inside the door, he could see through the large glass windows into two different autopsy suites.

"Two autopsies in one day?" In the room on the right, he could just make out the long dark hair of what had been a woman as two gowned figures wielded scalpels and saws around her. The occupants of the room on the left appeared to be a single doctor and a man laid out on the stainless steel table.

"It's a sad story." Oliver joined Cade in watching the macabre show. "She's his fiancée. Some rich couple or something. Their names were in the paper—Newton or something. Anyway, he apparently snapped last night and strangled her before dropping dead himself."

This was the society he'd fought for, Cade thought bitterly. The sort of place where you couldn't even turn your back on those you loved. At least in Afghanistan he'd known who wanted him dead.

"Any idea what killed him?' Cade asked after glancing over his shoulder to find Alex had disappeared.

"Too early to know. Some people here put bets on drugs, but they didn't seem the type. Just a couple days ago, I passed them over on 35th street, volunteering with that mobile soup kitchen that sits there some times. Seemed like they genuinely wanted to help."

"Wouldn't happen to be this soup kitchen, would it?" Alex inserted herself between them and held up a crumpled flyer triumphantly. "Found this in Mr. Mason's pocket."

Oliver took the paper from her and scanned it. "Yeah that's the one. I remember because they were handing out these fliers that day saying that Representative Prince himself would be there that evening to serve. As if those people cared about a stuffy politician who was probably going to show up for five minutes for a photo op. All they want to do is eat."

Cade was inclined to agree. Politics hadn't interested him much before he'd enlisted, and now that he was back home, he had even less of taste for them. Anybody who treated soldiers as chess pieces instead of people didn't deserve his respect.

"So we know Mason was near that area that same day since he had the flier. How does that help us?" There had to be something more to Alex's discovery. She seemed much too happy for so little information.

"It gives us our next stop." She shoved the paper into her own pocket. "How does soup for lunch sound?"

Something was definitely up. "Uh…"

"Fantastic. Oliver, thanks for all your help." She flashed the young doctor a quick smile, which didn't bear even the faintest resemblance to the occasional real one Cade had seen from her.

"Oh, you're welcome. Um, if I can do anything to help… I just mean, if you need anything at all…"

Alex didn't seem to notice as Oliver stammered all over himself. "Cade, let's go."

With an apologetic wave in Oliver's direction, he followed her out the door.

⌒

"Okay, spill," he demanded once they'd left the hospital behind. Alex pranced a few steps ahead of him. It appeared they'd be walking instead of taking a taxi this time.

"What?" she asked innocently, and it might have been convincing if the faint hint of a smile hadn't followed her question.

"The syringe contents, the soup kitchen, whatever else you found in Mason's jacket… You're much too happy about free soup for there not to be something else."

"This whole thing is brilliant," she admitted as her eyes widened in excitement. "The liquid in the syringe was a combination of chemicals I've never seen before. Some sort of poison obviously. It's quite volatile, hence the skin decomposition we noted on Bishop. It also contains large amounts of chemicals that could induce a state of psychosis."

"So like an LSD trip?"

"Something like that," she agreed before jaywalking around an SUV whose driver laid on his horn.

Cade waved in apology and followed her. "But that still doesn't tell us why they decided to use the poison when there were much simpler ways to finish him."

"Because they're testing it." Alex tapped the screen of her phone and raised it to show him. The dark headline stood out against the backlit screen. *Georgetown Lovers Dead In Murder-Suicide.*

"While you were talking to Oliver, I looked up the names of the bodies to come through the morgue in the last two weeks who weren't obviously killed by an incompetent doctor. Besides those two, I found two other likely candidates. I used Oliver's log-in information to look up the autopsy results, and the first two bodies were in horrible shape. One even gnawed his own arm off."

"You're saying whoever is doing this is murdering random people and then adjusting the formula based on the results? That's... that's..."

"Brilliant, I know."

"Not exactly the word I was looking for."

"That's because you have no imagination. The first two victims were homeless. Didn't even make the news. They were chosen because no one would notice. Now, if they're still working to get the formula just right, you have to wonder why they would target someone as conspicuous as that couple who is a fixture on the society pages or Nathan Bishop who was well-known and loved in his community."

"It doesn't make sense," he conceded as they turned down 35th street. To his left stood a small white church, and on his right, a hill spotted with tombstones. Perfect. As if he needed ambience to make their conversation even creepier.

"It doesn't make sense unless you realize they may have made a mistake." Alex crossed this smaller street without even looking, and when no horns sounded, Cade looked over his shoulder and followed her. "The first two victims make sense. Nathan Bishop makes sense because he had something they wanted. But Max Newton and his fiancée don't fit. What if they weren't the intended target?"

Cade was saved having to come up with an answer by their arrival at the soup stand. It was nothing more than a small table set up outside a white van with small black lettering that read *Mobile Soup Kitchen* and larger lettering and a picture that announced the sponsor as Steven Adams, who Cade recognized as the Secretary of Homeland Security. Cade resisted the urge to roll his eyes. Between this guy's picture on the side of the van and that Jonathan Prince guy making appearances to hand out soup, feeding the homeless seemed like just another publicity stunt.

Three volunteers stood behind the table, talking with and serving the dozen or so people who had crowded around. Their disheveled appearance, body odor, and the way they inhaled the soup felt like a punch of guilt in Cade's gut. It served him right for complaining about how good he had it.

Alex surprised him by waiting patiently until most of the patrons had dispersed, either to rest against the cemetery's fence and finish eating or to other locations. Only then did she step forward and, almost as if becoming a different person, offered a timid smile at the only female volunteer.

"Um, excuse me," Alex said in a small voice that had him doing a double take. "I'm sorry to bother you, but I was hoping you could help me find someone."

"I'll do my best." The girl, probably a college student judging from her attire of jeans and sweatshirt and messy pile of hair on her head, smiled brightly at Alex.

"Well, I was wondering if you'd ever seen this man around here." She held up her phone, and Cade caught enough of a glimpse to see she'd taken a picture of Mason's ID badge from the hospital. "My boyfriend and I," she jerked her head in Cade's direction, "ran into this man here before, and we hired him and his friend to do some work for us. We were so pleased we wanted to recommend them to some friends of ours, but we don't have a way to get in touch with them. We've been to every soup kitchen in the area, and no one seems to know them."

It shouldn't have surprised him, the effortless way she weaved the lie, but there was something about her sweet tone he just couldn't reconcile with the woman he'd come to know. Fortunately, the volunteer didn't know better.

"I've seen him around here once or twice." She gnawed on her bottom lip as she studied the picture. "I don't even know his name, but I've seen him hanging around Tiny."

"Yeah, Tiny." Alex glanced at Cade, and he took that as a sign to join in.

"Yes, that was his name." He stepped closer and pressed his side as close to Alex as she would allow. "Do you know where Tiny usually hangs out?"

"He does some occasional work for the cemetery." The girl nodded toward the green hills behind them. "Not that there's much to be done since it's falling apart. But Tiny does some odd jobs around there. Usually takes a break on the evenings he's working to come down here for something to eat."

"Great." Alex's face lit up. She jabbed him in the side, and he turned a grimace into a fake smile.

"Yeah, great," he muttered through clenched teeth.

"We'll come back tonight to see if we can catch him then. Thanks so much for your help." Alex continued her sickly sweet smile until she'd waved goodbye to the girl, and they turned their backs on the soup truck. "You are a horrible actor."

"A little notice would have been nice. You can't just start something like that and expect me to jump in the middle."

"It doesn't matter." Her voice was back to its usual smooth timbre, and her lips pressed into a tight line. Digging her hand into her pocket, she produced a key. "We got what we needed."

"And what is that?" The small silver key she held looked like it went to a padlock of some sort. Definitely not a door or car key.

"It must go to something in the cemetery, a shed or something. Mason and Tiny were connected, therefore the scalpel from the hospital and the dirt from a pit fit—not a pit so much as a grave. I also found small traces of granite in the bit of dirt from the rope, probably from a headstone. And I wasn't intentionally keeping that from you, but I had to run it through the mass spectrometer."

"Anything else you want to tell me before I agree to break into a cemetery with you this evening?"

Her nose crinkled slightly in a weak attempt to hide her grin. "You've already agreed."

"I don't remember saying that."

"You didn't have to. You enjoy this—being part of a team again."

It was perhaps the first time he'd heard any semblance of doubt in her voice, and for some unknown reason, he felt the need to reassure her. "It's nice to be part of something, though I'm not sure how much of a team it is since I'm deadweight."

"Your contribution to this investigation has given me a different perspective on working with a partner," she admitted slowly. "If neither of us manages to get killed before this is over, we should discuss a more permanent arrangement."

"I've already moved in. Sounds pretty permanent to me."

Alex stopped abruptly in the middle of the sidewalk. When he turned back, some of her icy façade had melted. "Seriously, Cade, I don't want to force you into doing something you don't want to do."

"I really can't see you being able to *force* me to do anything."

"Eh, maybe not physically, but there are still so many other options…" She trailed off into an almost dream-like state, and he shuddered to think what she was dreaming up for him.

"The point is, I've seen three bodies so far, put out a fire, and pretended to be your boyfriend for two minutes. None of that has put me off."

"You like danger."

I like you. It didn't feel right to say that, not with the chance that she might misconstrue it as something romantic. And he hadn't missed that she'd implicitly suggested being her boyfriend was dangerous. He decided on humor instead of the truth. "I like cheap rent."

"Which reminds me," she began as she started walking again, "don't hold your breath on the mopping."

He didn't hold back a laugh.

CHAPTER SEVEN

Alex liked this part of detective work more than all the time she spent in the lab. Of course, science was fascinating and necessary, and there was always so much to be learned. But no one stood over her shoulder in the lab to appreciate her brilliance or see her proved right.

Field work, on the other hand, provided her ample opportunity for showing off. People seemed to think it poor taste when she put it like that, but it was true. Time spent with Cade only cemented that for her. Cases were more fun when she had someone around to impress with her grand deductions.

She'd traded in her heels and tailored suits for black yoga pants, a black sweatshirt, which she'd turned inside out to obscure the white Metro PD logo on the front, and dark tennis shoes. Still, complete stealth seemed impossible since the moon was nearly full, and the faint glow of nearby streetlights occasionally interrupted the shadows. But if any of the people passing on the sidewalk below noticed two extra shadows milling among the tombs, they kept silent.

Her fingers brushed the key she'd shoved in her pants pocket for the hundredth time just to make sure it was still there. It would go to a small lock of some sort, possibly the caretaker's shed. Judging from the tall grass and weeds, which brushed against her shins, and the leaning granite in various degrees of shambles, the shed—if there was one—didn't get much use. That made it the perfect place to hide something.

"Over here." Cade's breath warmed her cheek as he materialized at her side then darted back into the shadows.

Of course he'd be adept at stealth. Her skills were far from basic, but there were some things that came naturally to a well-trained soldier. Perhaps, she hated to admit, she could even learn a few things from him. Of course that miniscule amount of knowledge paled in comparison to how much she could teach him.

She joined him in the cover of a willow tree at the top of a hill, lungs burning from the tense dash she'd just made in that direction. He wasn't even breathing hard.

Cade held up a hand to keep her silent, then gestured, with the wave of a single finger, to a small building at the bottom of the hill. It was difficult to make out as it was tucked away between two overgrown trees. Perfect.

With a nod, she instructed him to move.

The dry grass prevented them from sliding as they descended the hill, finally shielded from the street by the terrain. No signs of anyone who looked like a Tiny. By this time, he should have already visited the soup kitchen and gone on his way for the night. On occasion people surprised her, but as a whole, they were mind-numbingly predictable. Besides, she'd take her chances on encountering him with Cade leading the way.

"You don't think it's rigged, do you?" Cade tilted his head in her direction, but didn't take his eyes off the dilapidated shed.

"This isn't the Taliban, Captain Blackwell."

"It doesn't take a genius to rig a booby trap."

"Doesn't take a genius to recognize one either…or the lack of one."

She was, admittedly, somewhat oblivious to the emotional responses of others unless they directly pertained to a case. But when Cade's steady stride faltered beside her, an unfamiliar pinch of something—guilt?—made her cringe in the darkness.

"I shouldn't have said that?" Data for this sort of thing didn't exist in her brain. It might have been because she'd always been careless with her words, not caring who she wounded with the truth because it was, in fact, the truth.

"No, you shouldn't have." His words were close, but his voice sounded miles away. Back in Afghanistan likely.

Okay, a confirmation she'd said the wrong thing. What now? Did she apologize? How did people go through their lives caring so much? So tedious. But what if he left? She didn't want that.

"Stop thinking so much and get the key out," Cade instructed as he left her at the shed's door and circled the perimeter.

The padlock, obviously newer than anything else in this

graveyard, gave way after a single turn of the key. She didn't bother with gloves as she unhooked the lock and eased the creaking door open. Then Cade was there, blocking her entrance with his forearm. A protest was on her lips, but he quelled it with a look.

"I go first."

She didn't bother with any arguments as she took a step back to appease him. Now here was a man capable of surprising her. Not because he'd insisted on going first—his sense of duty demanded it—but that he was here with her at all. She'd known him for three days. Almost double the amount of time it took for everyone else to leave. To find out there was a tradeoff with her genius.

Her sister wouldn't like it, not at all. But if she could keep Cade a secret from Charlotte for a while longer, this partnership might stand a chance.

Cade stuck his head out of the shed. "All clear."

Alex entered the wooden building and immediately noted the precise creak of the floorboards as well as the dried dirt staining the shovel hanging on the wall. A bit obvious, but she would have been a little disappointed if this excursion hadn't included digging in a cemetery in the middle of the night.

"They've buried something recently," she said for Cade's benefit as he studied the various tools on the wall. "Help me get this board up so we can see what's underneath."

Cade managed to pull the board up on his first try by wedging a rusted crow bar underneath. He kicked the board to the side with the toe of his shoe and knelt beside her to examine the piece of paper that just stuck out of the dirt underneath.

"It's just another one of those stupid soup kitchen fliers." He sort of groaned a sigh and drug his fingers through his hair.

She pulled the paper from the dirt and used her phone as a flashlight to illuminate it enough to read. It looked nearly identical to the one she'd found in Mason's jacket at the morgue except for the presence of doodling on the back. Except it wasn't just a bored man's random drawing. The pen that had drawn this stopped and started, as if the artist was considering his next move. Clearly not the work of a master, but there had been some rhyme or reason behind the sketch.

"A map," she whispered. When she looked up, she was nearly nose to nose with Cade who'd been observing the drawing as well. "What do you say to a treasure hunt? Maybe a little light digging?"

His breathy, disbelieving laugh fanned her face before he sat back on his heels. "I was afraid you might say that."

"You were hoping I would." The darkness couldn't hide everything, and the hum of energy he emitted was nearly palpable. He was enjoying this almost as much as she was. "Grab the shovel over there, and let's go."

It took them half an hour and one false destination to find the real burial site. Another fifteen minutes of Cade's digging passed before the shovel struck something more solid than the dark soil.

"If this is a coffin, I hope they realize you're the brains of the operation and haunt you instead."

"If this coffin is only three feet deep, this body deserves to be disturbed," she muttered as she shoved the map in her pocket and joined him in digging around the outline of a box in the dirt.

Once they'd unearthed the small metal box, Cade used the shovel to break the small padlock from the lid. Alex eagerly pried the lid open and gasped.

Rolls of cash lined the edges of the box while two envelopes took center stage. She immediately deduced the contents of one as the item Nathan Bishop had kept in his book safe. With careful fingers, she broke the seal on that envelope and began reading.

The author was well educated with careful penmanship evidenced by the single 'M' that served as the signature. The rest of the letter was typed, had been printed on a laser printer on high quality stationary, and embossed with the seal of the United States House of Representatives.

"What does your letter say?" Cade's eyes narrowed as he scanned the contents of the other envelope.

"This is big," she whispered. Much bigger than she had bargained for. Nice to have a proper mystery for once instead of the same dull murders she'd solved of late for the police. "It's a letter from Representative Jonathan Prince's office to Representative Hutchins that outlines the perks Hutchins would receive for supporting Prince's appointment to Secretary of Homeland Security."

But why did Bishop have this letter? Maybe someone had turned it over to him as a means of confessing a guilty conscience. Certainly the Reverend must have recognized it held some significance since he thought to store it in a hidden safe. Instead of going to the police with it, he'd called her instead. If she'd been an hour or two earlier with their meeting, she might have gotten a look at the letter Bishop wanted her opinion on before the thugs got there to extract it. And if Bishop hadn't called her, she probably wouldn't be involved with this case at all. Maybe Cade wouldn't have hung around without something this interesting to hold his attention...

"We've already got a Secretary of Homeland Security. It's that guy that sponsors the soup kitchens—Steven Adams."

She'd nearly forgotten Cade was still there, that she was supposed to be having a conversation with him. "Not for much longer, we won't. I don't know how, but..."

"I think I do." Cade held up his letter, handwritten instead of typed and stained with dirt and smudges. "This is from Tiny to Mason. I can't read some of it, but it looks like the third guy in their group wants to take matters into his own hands."

Alex grabbed the letter from Cade and began to read. Apparently, the third mercenary—someone named Dieter—was having second thoughts on turning Bishop's letter over to their boss—hence why it was buried in the cemetery rather than in the hands of their sponsor. Dieter planned to tell their benefactor that Mason had taken the letter and failed to turn it over while he and Tiny used the letter to blackmail Jonathan Prince for his involvement in an apparent terrorist plot, leaving Mason to take the heat from their boss. Tiny apparently hadn't agreed with Dieter's decision.

She read the last two paragraphs three times before she understood the details of Prince's plot.

"The soup kitchens. They're going to use the poison they've been developing to mass poison different parts of the city at the same time."

Cade paused long enough for Alex to count to ten before he responded. "I know you're going to say this is obvious, but why would they want to kill the people who would be eating at the soup kitchens?"

"Well, they won't be able to prove it's the soup kitchens, of course, at least not immediately. That's why they've taken their time developing this poison. Injected, it acts quickly, but ingested, I imagine it could take at least half an hour to take effect. It's why the Newtons don't fit the victim pattern. These guys were testing a small amount in some of the soup, and the Newtons happened to be the unlucky ones. If they succeed in this, you'll have a psychotic mob stumbling around, highly suggestible while under the influence, who will cause unimaginable chaos and then die. Then Prince will undoubtedly produce proof that the current Secretary Adams and his soup kitchens were responsible, thus branding Adams as a terrorist and leaving the office open for him to step in as a hero."

"I'd be impressed, but that's terrifying." Cade sat back on his heels. She felt his eyes on her, but couldn't make out the details of his expression. "What are we going to do? This is over our heads. We don't know when they're planning to do this."

"I'll give these letters to Grisham in the morning," she agreed reluctantly. But not before she'd extracted every bit of information she could from them. "It's still up to us. It'll take forensics days to verify this letter from Prince's office is real and just as long to track down Tiny or this Dieter. And I don't even want to think how they'll go about looking for this 'M' that signed the letter. We might not have that much time."

"What do you want to do?"

"Our band of hired guns is starting to turn on each other. For some reason, Dieter wants to cut Mason out of his plan to double cross Prince or whoever hired them. If we can get to Mason, we might be able to find more information." It was a delicate situation when negotiating strained relationships. Not her best area, which was why she planned to avoid actual talking if at all possible.

"He should be working at the hospital tonight," Cade offered. "Maybe you could get Oliver to let us in again?"

"We won't learn anything by talking to him." She stood and dusted her pants off. "We'll pay his house a visit tomorrow while he's at work. That should be sufficient time for me to get this evidence to Grisham and get the ball rolling on a search warrant."

"I don't think you're qualified to carry out a warrant."

"No, but it makes them feel better about the evidence I bring them."

They stole out of the cemetery as quietly as they'd entered and decided to forgo a cab in favor of walking home. She needed the time to order her thoughts, and there was no use arousing a taxi driver's suspicions given their dark clothes and dirty appearance. Not to mention the box full of money Cade carried under his arm.

Alex fingered the letters in her pocket, trying to decide how much of an explanation to give Grisham when she dropped them off. Even he would figure it out eventually, but it might be nice to have a head start. One wrong move by the police and they'd lose this lead.

No, the pressure lay solely on her…and Cade if she didn't wake up to find he'd moved out. This was a lot to ask.

She chanced a glance at him. Strong, stoic, yet clearly damaged. He was simply trading one war for another.

He caught her looking and offered a forced half smile that did nothing to convince her he was confident in their agenda.

If she was honest, neither was she.

Cade's muscles were stiff with the pleasant ache of use when he awoke just before noon the next day. Consecutive days of little sleep and high adrenaline had caught up with him around four that morning, and he'd left Alex sitting in her chair in favor of his bed.

But he wasn't at all surprised when he descended the stairs to find her in the same spot he'd left her. Her fingers curled around a steaming cup of coffee provided the only indicator she'd moved at all. It was amazing she could still sit upright after so many days of little sleep and little sustenance, but he'd have no chance of convincing her to eat since food hadn't magically appeared in their fridge or pantry.

"I think around six, don't you?" Alex said between sips of her coffee, as if he'd walked into the middle of a conversation. Cade flopped into the chair opposite her.

"What's around six?" He was still too tired to play coy with her non-sequitur, though he wasn't sure if it qualified as a non-sequitur if there wasn't a previous conversation for it to follow. Cade eyed her coffee with envy. Why was it such a long way to the kitchen?

"When we're paying a visit to Mason's address."

"Oh. Right. Of course." For a brief moment, he'd forgotten the lives of hundreds of people rested in their hands… his very shaky hand. For some unknown reason, his right hand refused to be steady this morning. So much for being cured. "Did you take those letters to Grisham?"

She nodded. "He came by to pick them up a couple hours ago. I had to talk him out of taking Prince into custody for the moment, though. If we tip our hand too early, we'll never know who's really behind this."

That's why Alex was in charge of this rodeo. If it were up to him, Prince would already be locked away for a long time. "So we're just going to wait around until this evening, and you're okay with that?"

"What else do you want me to do?" Her fingers drummed absently against the cup. Except it probably wasn't absently. Everything about her said control and calculation.

"I don't know." How could she just sit there? He stood and paced the length of the room in his socked feet. "You're the genius. You figure something out."

"It's all science, Cade, and you have to wait for the optimum time to end an experiment. Cut it off too early and you'll miss the most important piece."

She was right, of course, and he hated it.

"You're angry," she stated with no emotion as she set her cup aside and crossed her long legs.

"Yes." Why shouldn't he be? He had no idea what to do next,

but he wasn't a genius. Surely there was something that could be done right now.

"More than you were last night, about the booby trap," she continued. Curiosity lifted her tone slightly.

He didn't want to think about that. Mostly because what she'd said had been true, and she had said it without regard for his feelings. Wasn't that what he'd wanted all along? Not to be coddled or treated differently because of what happened? But he *was* different, though he was just starting to realize it.

"Yes," he replied in a tone so defeated he barely recognized it as his own. "More than last night."

"You hate feeling useless, which is how you view this waiting period."

"If you don't act, people die." The effort to keep the tremor out of his voice was in vain.

"And sometimes even if you do." She picked up her coffee cup again and turned it bottom up to finish it. "You know, that would have tasted a lot better with some milk."

"Fine." He stalked to the stairs with the intent of changing his clothes. He'd get milk but only because he really wanted a bowl of cereal, and eating every meal out was overrated. Anything to get out of the house, even if it was just grocery shopping. "I'll go to the store this time, but don't think I won't make you go next time."

Two hours later, Cade lugged six bags of groceries up their front steps. Army ranger camp had nothing on a couple mile walk with his hands going numb from the way the bags hung off his arms. What they had in common was how the exertion calmed him to the point he thought he could put up with almost anything.

Anything included the burnt rubber smell coming from the kitchen. After depositing the bags on the counter with a huff, Cade glanced at the mess on the table. Alex's dark head was bowed over some sort of petri dish, which seemed to be the source of the smell.

"My wallet's next to the microwave. Take some cash for the groceries." She didn't even look up.

Cade paused, waiting for her to at least make eye contact, but when she showed no sign of further acknowledging him, he retrieved her wallet from the far end of the counter. He kept one eye on her as he opened it in case this was a trick, but she seemed as disinterested as ever.

He didn't know what a crime-solving genius's wallet should look like, but Alex's was disappointingly simple. Very spartan and organized with no receipts or notes, each slot filled with a card of some sort. Oh. A diamond platinum card, the kind they wouldn't even send him solicitations for. He discreetly slid the card up enough to verify her name was at the bottom, then laughed softly to himself for being so silly.

A crisp twenty was neatly folded in the back pocket, and he'd decided to grab it and put the wallet down when her driver's license caught his eye. Alexandria Suzanne Holst, born July 16, 1983. So only thirty-two, which meant she'd graduated college a couple years early. Not surprising. Five feet, eight inches tall and weighing one hundred thirty-five pounds. He didn't recognize the address listed. Even with all her basic stats, he still knew next to nothing about her except she took a ridiculously good looking picture.

"Hasn't anyone ever told you it isn't polite to look through a lady's things?"

"Good thing you're not a lady." Still he snapped the wallet closed and returned it to the counter. She didn't look up, but he could read her smile in the subtle shift of those sharp cheekbones.

It took less time than he would've liked to put away the groceries. When he'd finished, the clock still read only 2:00. What to do until they left for Mason's house? He needed a distraction.

Leaving Alex and the worst of the smell in the kitchen, he planted himself on the couch and turned the TV on. After flipping through soap operas and infomercials, something familiar caught his attention.

"Oh look, the Princess Bride's on. Isn't that ironic?" He mashed the button on the remote to raise the volume.

"Why is that ironic?" Alex called from the kitchen. "And could you turn that down?"

"Because you made a reference to it yesterday," he replied, choosing to ignore her second question. It was his house, too, and if she could burn the curtains down and produce acrid smells in their kitchen, he could certainly turn the TV up.

"No, I didn't." The sound of a chair screeching across the kitchen floor preceded her appearance in the doorway, now holding a blow torch and wearing safety glasses. He really wished he hadn't see that. "Why would I do that? And that's the incorrect use of 'ironic'."

"Fine," he groaned, "a coincidence."

"Nope." She popped the 'p' and entered the living room only to stand directly in front of the TV. "Coincidence is a lazy man's excuse, and the universe is rarely so lazy."

Cade forced a smile. "Excellent. So God must want you to take a break from those awful smelling experiments and watch this classic movie."

Her nose wrinkled like a petulant child. "Why in the world would I do that?"

"Because it might save your life someday… like right now. Because if you don't move and let me do something mind-numbing like watch this movie, I just might snap."

Her eyes lit up as if he'd just said the perfect words to activate her switch. She disappeared into the kitchen, then reappeared moments later sans torch and glasses but with a notebook and pen instead.

"What are you doing now?" Maybe he should have insisted she continue in the kitchen. At least she would be out of his way.

"Taking notes." Alex plopped down at the far end of the couch, then proceeded to sprawl out so her feet were almost in his lap. It was bad enough that her presence seemed to take up the whole room with her easy confidence, but now she was physically taking up space as well.

"Do you always take notes when you watch TV?"

"You never know what might come up in a case."

He didn't press for more of an explanation. The movie was at one of his favorite parts—the sword fight between the man in black and Inigo. Cade tried to relax, to lose himself in the story, but Alex's manic scribbling beside him was distracting. He could just see her in his peripheral. She'd sat on his good side on purpose.

"Can you stop?"

Her pen froze. "What?"

"The writing. Can you stop the writing and just enjoy the movie?"

"This movie's ridiculous. It was obvious that neither of them were left-handed. It's hardly a surprise." She gestured at the screen where, Cade realized, he'd missed the entire sword fight.

"Can you turn your brain off for two minutes and just watch?" When she didn't offer an immediate retort, he sank back into the cushions and returned his attention to the TV.

He'd almost forgotten she was there until she made a noise of disgust and dropped her notebook. "For Heaven's sakes. Iocane powder? Cade, this is—"

The words died on her lips when she saw the look he gave her. Battled-hardened soldiers had withered under his steely eyes, and while she didn't exactly shrink back, she did shut up, which he considered an enormous success.

But she didn't look away. Even when he'd turned his attention back to the movie, he felt her eyes on him, probing every detail. What would she see? The tightness in his shoulders from the exceptionally bad dream he'd had last night? A certain set to his mouth that told her he hadn't had a romantic attachment or kissed anyone since before Afghanistan? The shaking of his hand that marked him as an invalid in ways his psychological wounds didn't?

Just as the first time, the thought of being seen by her was a terrifying thrill. Nothing was safe or off limits. He'd always considered himself an honest person, but this took things to a different level. Unfortunately, it wasn't reciprocated. And why would it be? What could he possibly hope to understand about her?

He knew he was doing a better job than most people, if only because he appreciated her complexity. Grisham clearly needed her for her work, and Detective Walker despised her for reasons he suspected bordered on jealousy. Even Oliver, who obviously was head over heels for Alex, didn't seem to offer what she really needed. Not just an audience, but a friend.

Everyone had expectations of her, and he knew what it felt like to carry that weight. Yes, she was a genius who got excited about murders and seemed to say exactly what crossed her mind as if she couldn't possibly hold back the truth, nor would she want to. But she had to be human somewhere underneath all that. The way she'd pulled back when she gauged his reaction to her careless words about booby traps suggested she wasn't completely heartless.

He and Alex remained in those positions for the duration of the movie with her eyes rarely looking away from him and his mind never far from her. What a pair they made.

"What did you do when you lived alone?" he asked as the credits rolled across the screen, and he finally gave himself permission to look at her.

"Who says I lived alone?" She tucked her feet under her, then arched her back in a stretch. There was a sort of feline grace about her that made him think she probably always landed on her feet.

He didn't know what to say next since he'd been so sure she must have spent much of her life in isolation until now. "You set fire to household decor and grow potentially toxic things in petri dishes, and I don't even want to know about the blow torch. I can't imagine you've had a lot of roommates."

Her delicate features morphed into an expression that made him want to laugh though it jabbed him hard in the gut. A hopeful sort of expression, with her brows tilted in a way that screamed sadness—which he never would have noticed about anyone before he spent time with her—but with the faintest ghost of a smile on her lips. She'd been alone for some time, and, though she would probably never say it, she was happy to have him there.

It struck him as odd that she remained silent, letting him draw his own conclusions and never refuting or confirming. He might have thought she was simply being coy, but those upturned eyes told him differently. She was encouraging him to use her methods, to watch and catalog.

So he did, until all the staring and not talking began to make him uncomfortable.

"It's nearly five," he announced as he stood and stretched. "I'm taking a shower before we leave. Maybe you want to decontaminate the kitchen?"

She let out a breath, visible only by the slight shift of her shoulders. Had she been holding it this whole time? He mentally face-palmed himself. He'd thought they were having a moment while she was probably calculating how long she could hold her breath and which extremities went numb first.

Still, she did mimic her earlier smile as she stood and walked toward the kitchen. He just shook his head. Alex might be human, but it was buried underneath a lot of baggage. But with hundreds of lives on the line and a madman—or three—running loose, now wasn't the time to start digging.

CHAPTER EIGHT

"This is breaking and entering." Cade hissed as he slid through the window after Alex and landed softly on the wood floor. He tugged his shirt back down and rubbed the bruise he'd have on his side where the window sill had dug into his skin.

The dimming outdoor light cast her eyes in shadow, but he could still see she was scowling. "What exactly did you think we were going to do when we decided to visit the house of a potential mass murder who's supposed to be at work?"

Fair enough, but it still needed to be stated. Not that he hadn't done his fair share of trespassing in the army, but it had been sanctioned by the US government. Despite Alex's ego, she wasn't the government. "We should just call the police."

"And tell them what?" she mouthed back, just barely audible. "That we've just broken in? You're not very good at this." Alex took her shoes off and hooked the heels over one finger. "Just follow me and stay quiet. I only want to search the place, and then we'll be on our way."

They moved silently through the kitchen, into a small living area. Even taking short precise steps, Cade still nearly stumbled over furniture and boxes, his heart pounding as he righted himself. At least in Afghanistan he'd had a weapon in the event of a surprise. His Sig Sauer P228—not his actual service weapon, though an identical one—lay in his bedside table at home. Next time he travelled with Alex, he'd be sure to stick it in his waistband.

Only the soft hum of electronics and his shallow breathing accompanied Alex's nearly balletic movement around the room. Leaping from place to place, crouching to examine surfaces of tables and shelves, she moved with an indiscernible purpose. Though he tried to make himself useful, Cade saw nothing remarkable about the shelves lined with too many action movies and not enough books, or the collection of beer cans that adorned every flat surface in the room. Just like almost every other bachelor pad. They'd broken in for nothing.

"Someone was here. Recently." Alex's lips were at his ear without warning, the warmth of her breath making the hair on his arms stand up. "Two of those cans were half full and cool to the touch. Same brand as Grisham found outside Nathan Bishop's residence, by the way."

So it was. But it was hardly the treasure they were searching for. "This is pointless. Just let Grisham search the place. They can turn it upside down."

"They hardly have enough information for a warrant."

"They would if you'd give it to them." His louder whisper carried in the still house, and Alex glared before answering him at a lower volume.

"I don't like to share my theories until all the evidence has been examined."

"What? Are you actually afraid of being wrong?"

Even in the dark, he could see the roll of her eyes. "No. I'm afraid of little brains that will start to twist evidence to fit a theory rather than being objective. I'm saving you all from yourselves."

"Right." Humble as always. "What about those two rooms then?"

Before them lay two closed doors, and Alex gave him a meaningful look.

"Someone's hiding something."

Cade frowned.

"Well, how often do you close doors when you live alone? One of those is probably a bedroom, so a room he uses often. People who live alone don't close doors unless they have something to hide."

Well, when she put it that way, it seemed obvious. "Maybe he didn't make his bed."

Alex couldn't be bothered to comment because she'd pressed her ear against the door on the left. Another joke wasted on her. She held up a hand as he approached, and he instinctively stopped all forward progress. They remained perfectly still until Alex perked up at something she must have heard beyond the door.

After a flurry of complicated hand signals, Cade thought he

understood their next move, though he certainly didn't agree with it. Alex wanted to enter that room while he breached the other one. Splitting up when neither of them had a weapon seemed ill-advised at best, but telling Alex that, even if he'd been allowed to speak, was impossible. So he positioned himself as her mirror image, with his ear pressed to the other door and his hand—covered by his shirt-tail so he didn't leave fingerprints—wrapped around the handle.

Alex mouthed the countdown. *One. Two. Three.*

Rather than burst in with weapons drawn—since he didn't, in fact, have a weapon—Cade pulled the door open just enough to slide inside, hoping to silently surprise anyone who might be waiting on the other side. When he wasn't immediately attacked and didn't hear Alex call for help from the other room, he let out his held breath.

On the next inhale, he gagged.

In his fervid search for an attacker at eye level, he'd missed the dark mass on the floor nearly behind the bed on his initial scan. Flies buzzed in his ears as he doubled over, then stumbled back out the door.

He must have made some noise—though he couldn't hear anything over his heart roaring in his ears—because Alex was at his back immediately. Her fingers dug into his shoulders as she pulled him upright, and the sharp bite of pain centered him again. That smell, one of rotting flesh, in a small, dark space had sent him spiraling into the edge of a flashback. The blackness at the edge of his vision cleared marginally as he blinked Alex into focus.

"Are you all right?" Her tone indicated she'd asked him more than once, but this time he managed to nod. With a brief nod of her own acknowledgement, she released him and rushed into the room he'd stumbled out of.

Slow and even breaths parted his lips as he calmed himself down. Just the perfect storm of circumstances, that's all. On their own, he wasn't scared of bodies or the dark or even small spaces. Together they transported him back to mountain caves where his fellow soldiers lay wounded or dying while they waited helplessly for rescue.

But he wasn't in Afghanistan. He was here. With Alex. And this case had just gotten a lot bigger.

With mental preparation, Cade stepped into the room again and found her kneeling over the body. She didn't look up, so he cleared his throat to make sure she knew he was there. No need to worry about noise now. If there had been someone else in the house, he'd certainly scared them away with his reaction to the body.

"You can stay outside if you'd like."

Sometimes he hated how she spoke with no emotion. How was he supposed to know if she was angry or disappointed? Probably not sympathetic.

"I said I was fine." As if his insistence would make it more true.

"Not really, you're not." From her kneeling position, she looked over her shoulder at him. "When I reached you, your pulse was racing, eyes unfocused. You were fine when I saw you seconds before. Either you were exposed to a fast-acting hallucinogen, or you had some sort of PTSD symptom. A flashback obviously."

He knew what she meant now, when she'd told him people were sometimes angry at her deductions. That anyone could see what he'd tried to hide for months made him feel exposed and vulnerable. This was different than her deducing all those theoretical things about him because it served as confirmation that they were all true. His first instinct was to lash out in anger. Reining it in proved to be easier than he anticipated, largely because Alex had already moved on, and her all-seeing eyes were focused again on the body.

"Meet our good friend Mr. John Mason. I guess we'll be calling Grisham after all."

"Glad you've finally come to your senses." He pulled his phone from his pocket. Should he call 911? It wasn't exactly an emergency anymore. Maybe just look up Grisham's direct number. Alex probably had it.

"Not right now." An annoyed sigh came from Alex as she stood and yanked his phone from his hand. "Clearly we have to examine the scene before they get here and mess it up."

Clearly. Right. "You know, it is their job to deal with this sort of thing."

"And if they did it well, they wouldn't need me, would they?"

She made a good point. Still… "If you go to jail for this, I can't afford the rent on my own."

"I'm so glad your head's in the right place."

"Was that sarcasm? From you?" He held out his hand, waiting

for her to hand over his phone. When she reluctantly did, he returned it to his pocket. "Fine. You get fifteen minutes, and then I'm calling them. They've got an anonymous tip line, right?"

"Relax, Cade. Try to live a little. I'm sure Mr. Mason would share my sentiment if he weren't, well, dead."

"Definitely not the poster child for enjoying life."

As was fast becoming usual, Alex didn't reply to his attempted humor. Her attention was singularly focused on the body again. From her coat pocket, she pulled a pair of latex gloves and donned them almost as an afterthought. After their first few days together, it didn't even surprise him she carried things like that in her pockets. She grabbed the corpse's left hand and raised it so Cade could get a better look.

It looked like the normal hand of someone employed in manual labor—short nails and lots of callouses—with one significant exception. The left index finger was missing.

"Well?"

He drug his eyes from the hand to Alex's face, which stared up at him expectantly. Clearly he was supposed to be doing something, but he had no idea what.

"It's a hand..." That seemed safe enough.

Even in the dimness, he could easily see her shoulders rise and fall with a silent sigh. "Yes, but I was hoping you'd go a little deeper."

"He's missing a finger..." Oh. "The finger we found at Nathan Bishop's crime scene. Probably belonged to Mason."

"Obviously." Alex replaced the hand in the same position it'd been in. "And I told you the owner of that finger would be left-handed."

"How did you— Never mind. I don't want to know. Just hurry up and get what you need so we can get out of here."

"His murderer was far less patient than they were with Bishop."

Against his better judgment, Cade joined Alex in a crouch near the body. What could she have seen that told her that? Mason was facedown, but shallow, neat cuts were still visible along his forearms and through two slices in his t-shirt. Around those cuts, the tissue had already begun to decay, but much less so than Bishop's. That explained the horrific smell, at least.

"Tell me what you see," Alex instructed in a softer voice than he'd ever heard from her. It reminded him of hours earlier when she'd sat perfectly still and silently encouraged him to deduce all he could about her.

"Cuts along his arms and back are fairly shallow but must have been made with something very sharp because they're neat and precise. So, maybe a scalpel like the one that cut up Bishop?" He looked to Alex, and she nodded for him to continue. "The body's already starting to break down, but he couldn't have been dead for that long because you said the beer cans in the living room were still cold."

"Look closer." She pointed to a long slash on Mason's left arm. "Is that decay or something else?"

He forced himself to look closer, holding his breath as he did so. Finally, he sat back on his heels. "It does look more like a chemical burn. Do you think it's the same poison?"

"Yes." Alex stood and removed her gloves with a snap before

she shoved them into her pocket. "I think we have all we need here. We'll leave the way we came, and when we're ten minutes away, you can call the police."

"Wait. You don't want to look at anything else?" His analysis was superficial at best, but she hadn't added anything to it. There had to be more. He expected to miss it but couldn't believe she'd be satisfied with so little.

"I've got everything I need." She stepped past him. "I'll explain when we get home."

The first thing he did when they arrived back at Stanton Park was shove his handgun in the waistband of his pants. Alex reclined on the couch, watching him with disinterest as he pulled his shirt down to cover the weapon.

"Good, you follow then," she said suddenly, sitting forward and resting her hands under her chin.

"What?"

"Our next step. You got your gun so I assume you're ready."

"How can I be ready if you haven't told me where we're going yet?" For a genius, she could be unbelievably dense.

"To the address Mason drew in blood, obviously."

Obviously. "There was an address written in blood? And you didn't think that might be something worth mentioning?"

"Well, to be fair, I did give you a chance to observe for yourself."

"I'm not a detective, Alex."

"I know, but I'm working on that. Turns out the curve's steeper than I thought, but there's still some hope for you." She jumped from the couch and paced the length of the small living room, fingers steepled just under her chin. When she paused, she turned her eyes on him with laser focus.

"We're short on time, so I'll give you the summary. Mason was killed by one of the other two men who helped him murder Nathan Bishop, so either Tiny or Dieter. Like Bishop, he was tortured—probably for information, maybe for fun—but the man in charge of this murder lacked patience. The marks on Mason's body were much fewer than Bishop's, suggesting the murderer got tired of playing with him and ended it."

"Do you think he got what he wanted before Mason died?"

"Hard to say. Of course, we'll know soon enough when we visit the address." Cade frowned again. "Stop doing that look. Mason wrote part of an address in his own blood on the floor near his head. Clearly a message. Whoever murdered Mason is going to kill the other conspirator tonight at that address."

"You're guessing."

"I never guess."

By the set of her shoulders, the slight upward tilt of her chin, he knew she was serious. He could go dizzy from shaking his head in disbelief around her. "Where's this address?"

"Don't know exactly. Somewhere around the Golden Triangle. He wrote 'Po' and drew a triangle."

For a brief moment, Cade considered voicing how crazy it all was. The Golden Triangle wasn't a small place as it encompassed most of DC's central business district. A colossal waste of time to go to that part of town without a clue who they were looking for or where exactly they would find them. But if anyone could work it out, it would be Alex.

So he settled for something just as absurd. "Well, what are we waiting for then?"

"Is that what you're wearing?"

Out of all the things that had left Alex's mouth, that question surprised him most. She'd never sounded so...normal before. He looked down at the same pair of jeans, gray t-shirt and black jacket he'd worn all day.

"Yeah, sorry. All my serial killer hunting clothes are at the cleaners."

She smiled as she strolled to the stairs. "All right. I'll dress to match you then."

After disappearing up the stairs, Alex reappeared in the living room moments later. Jeans and a dark t-shirt were barely visible beneath her tailored trench coat. Between the fit of the coat and the black heels she wore—why women insisted on wearing those shoes and then complaining all night that their feet hurt was beyond him—she managed to retain an air of sophistication despite her otherwise unassuming look. So long as she didn't open her mouth, people might assume she was another young professional out for a night on the town.

A compliment was on the tip of his tongue when she marched up to him and yanked his handgun from the back of his pants. Too stunned to immediately react, he watched her study the weapon. She dropped the fully loaded magazine into her palm, examined the number of rounds, then put it all back.

It bothered him more than he could explain to have someone else handle his weapon. The smirk she offered as she handed it back didn't help.

"Don't try that again," he growled as he slid the cold muzzle of the gun against his back.

"I don't need to. The first time was too easy."

"Next time I'll put you on your back faster than you can blink." Cade didn't make empty threats.

"Next time, it might not be me taking it from you. Now come on. We've got a cab waiting out front."

CHAPTER NINE

She'd know it when she saw it. Something hidden in plain sight. Alex stood with her back pressed against the wall of a less crowded bar and surveyed the masses milling the streets in front of them. So hard to think with all this stimulation. A quiet place would be nice, but that was impossible to find in this area at this time of night.

Cade stood guard at her left shoulder, glaring down any men who dared to toss her a second glance. Admittedly she hadn't noticed why the first several had given the two of them a wide berth, but once she caught Cade straightening his posture and popping his jaw, she understood.

See. Too many distractions. Go back to what was certain. Mason had written the word 'po' and drawn the triangle. The triangle was the area they were currently standing in—the Golden Triangle. But 'po'?

Likely Chinese. Or at least Southeast Asian. In Chinese philosophy, the *po* referred to the second part of a soul—the *yin*—the part that remained with the corpse of the deceased. She supposed at the very least, it was an appropriately morbid last thing to write if you were dying.

There had to be something here. She shoved off the wall and began walking toward the more run-down part of the street. A couple of small bars and restaurants in decent shape, but abandoned store fronts intercalated on either side of them.

"You didn't say you were moving," Cade huffed close to her ear. He must've jogged to catch up to her.

"You're not my bodyguard. Make yourself useful and look."

"I *am* looking."

Good grief… "Not at me. Look for clues."

Wait.

She pulled to a sudden stop, and Cade fell into her, grabbing her around the waist to keep them both upright. He released her immediately, but she barely noticed. Alex saw nothing but the faint lines of a Chinese character etched into one of the abandoned building's dusty windows.

With lightning speed, she pulled out her phone, typed the word into the browser, and held the device up for Cade to see. "This is *po*. The symbol matches one of the two etched in that window over there."

"Amazing," he breathed, looking from her phone to the window and back with his wide brown eyes.

Curious. He'd spent three days with her and was still impressed by her skills. Unprecedented to say the least. And addictive. She'd begun to crave it.

"C'mon. We're going to have to find a back way in." Without waiting for his response, she moved toward the alley three storefronts down.

To his credit, Cade was right behind her, tension radiating from his body. Ever the soldier despite his insistence on downplaying his role.

She slunk down the alley past a homeless man—obviously former military, current heroin addict—and behind the row of buildings. The back alley was even narrower than the side one had been, not that it bothered her, but behind her, Cade inhaled sharply. Fighting another flashback.

But he said nothing, and they continued until she ducked behind a dumpster ten feet from the establishment's back door. That's when the smell hit her.

Sickly sweet with floral undertones and a certain thick richness to it. The tingling in her fingers confirmed her suspicions. Opium.

Stupid. The Golden Triangle wasn't just an area of DC. It was much more well-known as one of the top opium producing regions in Asia. Which had Mason meant? And how could she have missed that? Too many distractions.

"What now?" Distraction number one asked, nearly pressed against her back as they both peeked around the dumpster.

Right. Forget about the opium, forget about Cade. They were here to catch a killer. "We're going in that busted window there. This building's three stories tall. They won't do their business on the first floor to keep it looking abandoned. All we have to do it get inside and find Mason's accomplices."

"Right."

She hated when he did that. One word responses laced with sarcasm that even she could pick up on. Life was much easier when people just said exactly what they meant. "What?"

He hesitated. "Are you sure about this?"

"Of course I'm sure." She tried to look over her shoulder at him, but he stood too close. "What kind of question is that?"

"I'm sure it's going to be fine but—"

"Good. I'm also sure it's going to be fine."

"—except I'm not sure it's going to be fine."

He thought she was brilliant—unless that had been sarcasm as well—so why would he doubt her? "In the time that we've known each other—"

"It's only been three days."

Leave it to him to point out the insignificant. "In that time, have you known me to be wrong?" She could see it in his eyes. He only needed a little nudge to follow her off the cliff. It might even be nice not to jump alone for a change.

"No," he muttered.

"Right. And I'm 100% sure it's going to be fine."

"Nothing's 100%."

Ugh. This was why the military never got anything done. "Okay then. When you calculate the odds, come find me. I'll be inside."

That seemed all the push he needed. When she darted to the busted window and placed her hands on the sill, he was right there with her.

"Put your coat over the broken glass so you don't cut yourself." His voice was barely audible, softer than a whisper.

"I paid a lot of money for this coat. I'd rather dig the glass out of my hands."

"Oh for—here." Cade shrugged off his jacket and laid the dark material over the bottom of the window.

It wasn't especially thick, but it did the job, and Alex barley felt the crunch of glass beneath her hands as she vaulted over the sill and into the dark building. She stepped to the side on creaking floorboards, wincing as Cade followed her. They paused, waiting to see if anyone heard their entrance.

After a few seconds of silence, Alex moved toward the doorway of the room they'd entered through. From the floor above them, soft voices floated down the decrepit stairwell to her left. At least three men, one African American, two white. Such a shame she couldn't speak up to share that deduction with Cade.

She didn't have enough data to say conclusively that the men who'd killed Nathan Bishop were white—which was why she'd refrained from saying so—but that had always been her assumption. With Mason dead, it was very possible those were his associates at the top of the stairs, and one of them was getting ready to die.

It was tempting to just let justice run its course. What great loss would a murderer be? But if two of the three men were dead, that only left one to extract information from about the mass poisoning. It could certainly be done, but it was much easier to pit two suspects against each other. Even Grisham couldn't mess that up.

In her preoccupation with the men upstairs, she'd once again lost track of Cade. He apparently had an aversion to standing still. Not that she could see very well with only the weak glow of the streetlights to give the darkness a faded look, but his warmth no longer radiated near her and the faint sounds of his breathing had gone completely silent.

She closed her eyes, hoping to hone in on any sounds he made, but the sensory deprivation only served to strengthen her sense of smell. Once again, the sweetness of pure opium filled her nose, and a numb tingling began in her fingers. Just the edge of a high, but enough that she no longer felt the chill of the breeze through the busted windows. She sniffed, breathed it all deeper, and floated toward the stairs.

A hand clamped roughly over her mouth as she was jerked from the first stair and into Cade's arms. Her eyes wide, she could just make out the scowl on his face.

"Not without me," he breathed into her ear. With the effects of the drug rapidly dissipating, his warmth was the only thing keeping the chill at bay.

She nodded in response. How stupid could she be? Nine months without anything to slow her racing mind, a reprieve from the overstimulation, and she'd thought she'd kicked the habit. She'd managed to convince her sister and Grisham that she had.

But she couldn't do both. It was the drugs or the case. So she took a deep breath and held it in her lungs before following Cade up the stairs. His movements were so silent, so furtive, that she couldn't help but think if things didn't work out in their partnership, he could make an excellent burglar.

They paused four steps from the top, each of them in a crouch to stay out of sight of the men. One of them was laughing now at something one of the others said. It definitely didn't sound like a murder was about to be committed, but that didn't mean anything. They were discussing prices—of the opium presumably—but their tones didn't hold any tension or apprehension. Curious.

Cade looked over his shoulder at her and raised his brows in question. He wanted to know if she had a plan. Alex was grateful she didn't have to tell him she was making it up as she went along. Things usually worked better that way.

She slipped past Cade, bounded up the last four stairs and found herself face to face with three men who did not look pleased to see her.

"Police," she said, loud and clear without a thought as to what came after.

The men, who'd been staring at her with eyes wide and mouths agape, suddenly sprang into motion. One stumbled backward, toppling his chair with a cry of surprise while one of the others raked the drugs into a black bag. The third man's movement didn't register with her until the distinctive sound of the racking of a gun slide reached her ears.

Behind her, Cade cursed and grabbed her arm just as the wooden floor at her feet splintered in the wake of the bullet. He yanked hard, causing her to miss the first several stairs and land on her back in the same placed they'd been crouched moments before.

Another gunshot preceded the clomping of footsteps toward the stairwell. She managed to pull in another breath and shove Cade hard down the stairs.

"Down!" she yelled before rolling off the side of the stairs and crashing into a rickety table which immediately gave way. The blow took her breath away and stunned her for a moment. When the shock subsided, pain radiated up her arm.

Where was Cade? She tried to raise her head to make sure he hadn't taken a bullet, but it took considerable effort.

"C'mon!" His terse voice, laced with a no-nonsense authority gave her a small measure of relief.

She managed to roll off the table amid the hail of poorly aimed bullets, and caught up with Cade just as he ducked into the room they'd entered from. He grabbed her roughly around the waist and shoved her through the window.

Cade sprinted after Alex down the cramped alley, lungs burning and heart pounding but his feet light as ever. She took a sharp turn that he nearly missed until she reached back to pull him after her by his sleeve.

He nearly collided with her as she braced herself with her back against the larger alley's wall, chest heaving with gulps of air. They'd run three blocks from the abandoned building, and he could see the crowded main street from their position, so he let himself relax marginally beside her.

Their panting was the only sound that passed between them for several minutes. He couldn't believe he'd done that. Worse, he couldn't believe he'd *enjoyed* that.

"I may have slightly overestimated how fine it would be."

Alex's words hung in the air for a long second before the absurdity of it all crashed over him, and he doubled over in laughter. Before he could catch his first breath, Alex had joined him, her high, light laugh soaring over his baritone one. Her face, blurry through his tears of laughter, was open and nearly sparkling—or that could have been the light reflecting off her own tears. Either way, he hadn't thought she was capable of enjoying something so much, or at least not with an expression as common as laughter.

"You're an idiot," he finally choked out after catching his breath.

Her laughter died in her throat, and in that moment, he was afraid he'd offended her. Then she smiled, slowly, as if a real smile took genuine effort and wasn't just a reflex. "And yet you followed me. Once a soldier, always a soldier."

Hmm. She had him there. "Maybe you should quit telling people you're with the police. Doesn't seem like they take it too well."

"In my defense, they don't usually pull a .40 caliber on me."

"So those weren't our guys." It was as close as he would come to saying she'd made a mistake, at least at the moment.

"Not our guys," she agreed as she looked toward the main street.

Time to move on then, plot their next move. "I'm starving. You want to get something to eat since we came all the way down here?"

"Nothing for me."

A frown pulled his mouth down as he studied her pale face. "You were serious about not eating when you have a case."

Her eyes flicked back to him. "I need to be sharp. A little deprivation is good for the senses."

"Not so good for the body, though. You should get something here. How about a burger?"

"Told you, I'm not hungry."

"No, you told me you weren't eating. There's a difference."

"Not to me."

Of course not, but he dropped it. Three days together hardly made him responsible for her welfare. Together they stepped back into the craziness of the strip, and he scanned the signs for clues to a good burger joint. He'd almost decided to settle for a burrito instead when a small place near the end of the section of buildings across from them caught his eye.

The Raven. But what intrigued him more was the smaller lettering underneath. *Poe's Tavern*. Could it possibly… No, he wasn't Alex. Still, maybe she hadn't seen it yet.

"Alex, how educated do you think Mason was?"

"High school at best," she rattled off without looking at him. "Not very bright."

"So, it's possible he could misspell something simple. Something like Poe?"

Her head whipped around to follow his gaze. Cade's eyes flickered to her just in time to see her eyes widened and her mouth gape. Then he was being pulled across the busy street toward the tavern by the sleeve of his jacket.

"Excellent work, Cade."

It was as close to admitting she was wrong as he suspected he'd ever come. As long as he got to eat something, he didn't care.

The restaurant consisted mostly of a grungy bar area and a few booths, which probably looked better under a haze of smoke. He waited to follow Alex's lead and was relieved when she slid into an empty booth and undid the buttons on her coat. She'd put her back to the door, which surprised him but suited him just as well since he couldn't relax if he felt that exposed.

"What are we doing?" he asked after a waitress hurriedly took their drink orders.

"You're eating something greasy, I presume, and I'm watching," Alex explained as she looked everywhere but at him. He turned in the seat to look over his shoulder. "No, you don't look. We can't both look."

"Fine, but could you promise to warn me in time if a knife-wielding maniac is running toward me?"

"You're being ridiculous."

"Yeah, I might've thought so if we didn't just get shot at because you said everything would be fine." He lowered his voice as the waitress set their drinks down, then ordered a double cheeseburger and fries.

"You look fine to me," Alex said as the waitress walked away. "Better than fine actually." Her eyes, which hadn't stopped scanning the room since they entered, snapped to him.

Unprepared for the attention, he frowned. "What's that supposed to mean?"

"Your hand isn't shaking."

You're a freak, is what Cade heard. Still, he forced himself to leave his perfectly still hand resting on the table. It had taken her long enough to comment on it. "You're not the first person to notice that."

"Who was the first?" Her question had an edge to it, something he couldn't quite place.

"Some blond lady I met yesterday. Cornered me at a cafe. She basically said anything you could do, she could do better." He'd planned to tell her the whole of it, but when Alex's face fell with his every word, he changed his mind. Worried wasn't an expression he'd seen on her face, yet, but this was close.

"Weren't you going to tell me about her?" Every word slow and deliberate.

"I tried, but you weren't interested. Do you know her?"

She looked away, not to survey the room, but with an inward gaze that made him more curious than ever. "Yes, but we can't worry about her right now. Just promise me you'll let me know if she tries to contact you again."

Great. The woman had probably been on the FBI's most wanted list or something. "Do you want to know what she said about my hand?"

Alex looked back to him. "Your tremor in your hand is psychosomatic. I knew it early on. You subconsciously gave yourself a physical symptom to compensate for your psychological scars. Because without the tremor, you look like any other unwounded soldier, but deep down, you know you're not. You're not disfigured like so many of the war heroes that come home. Maybe you think you need the tremor to be worthy of the medal, of your status back home, especially since you keep insisting you were *only* a combat medic. But when it really counts, you're as solid as a rock."

He was silent for a long while. This was why people hated her. She told them things they didn't even know about themselves. As she'd said, his compensation was all subconscious, but it didn't make it any less true. She just had one thing wrong…

"In war, there's no such thing as an unwounded soldier."

Silence fell between them as she turned her attention back to the room, but Cade couldn't get her words out of his head. They hurt him, but he tried to push past the initial sting. She'd said he was solid when it counted. Alex trusted him even though she recognized how wounded he was.

The waitress brought his burger, and he was only two bites in when Alex stilled her fingers drumming on the table.

"What?" he asked with his mouth full.

"Someone just went in that first room in the back hallway. You can just see the door from here. It's one of our guys."

"How do you know?"

She rolled her eyes and slid out of the booth. "No time to explain. I'm going in there. Give me two minutes then follow me."

No chance to argue with her because she walked away from him. A huge sigh heaved his shoulders as he studied his watch. He'd give her one minute, not two. That was more than enough time for her to get into trouble.

Ignoring the rest of his burger, Cade watched the seconds tick away before he extricated himself from the booth. He immediately saw the door Alex meant. Thankfully it was down the same hallway as the restrooms so he wouldn't need an explanation for going that way.

Still, he glanced over his shoulder twice as he weaved past patrons and staff to stand in front of the door. Over the noise of the restaurant, he couldn't make out any distinguishing sounds from inside the room. Only one way to find out what was behind the door.

He reached back to reassure himself his gun was still in the waistband of his pants, then shoved the door open.

Three pairs of eyes turned toward him, Alex the closest and then two men—well, one was more accurately a giant. Both men held something in their hands. The large man—he had to be Tiny— clasped a pocketknife while the other appeared to wield something much smaller. Cade didn't have a chance to determine what it was because the man turned and elbowed out the glass in a window along the back wall, then climbed out.

Alex attempted to dart after him, but the big man snatched her up and pressed the knife to her throat.

"If you take a step, I'll cut her," he growled.

Cade had just begun to assess the likelihood of making the shot when the man doubled over with a grunt. Alex's elbow wasn't much, but it bought her enough time to duck out of her captor's arms and slide out the window.

The man righted himself and looked at Cade, both of them a little stunned. Then he followed Alex out the window, leaving

Cade little choice but to do the same.

The window led to another alley which dead-ended at a tall chain link fence. By the time Cade righted himself, he looked up to see the man pull Alex down from the fence and slam her to the ground.

Enough. With speed he hadn't used since combat, he sprinted the length of the alley and tackled the larger man to the ground. After a precarious few seconds when he feared the man might topple him, Cade managed to pin him to the ground.

"Wonderful job, Cade. Really couldn't have done it better myself." Alex had stood and now reclined against the brick wall as her fingers flew across her cell phone.

"Right," he grunted as the man shifted beneath him. "I don't think you could've."

"I told you, I'm perfectly capable of defending myself." Her voice was absent as she continued to type on her phone.

He looked down to the man beneath him, then back to her. She could see this, right? "Well, I hope you're also perfectly capable of calling the police because this is not the most comfortable position I've ever been in."

The huge man beneath him groaned in agreement, but there was no way Cade would let him up. And to attempt to wrench the knife from his hand might mean giving up his position. He pressed his fingers harder into one of the man's pressure points.

"I texted Grisham."

His surprise worked against him as the man on the pavement got in an elbow to his stomach, which forced the air from his lungs in a whoosh. Scrambling and clawing, the man shoved Cade back and made it to his knees before Alex pressed her heel against his back and shoved him face first to the ground. The point of her heel pressed a dent into the base of his skull until Cade could resume his position atop the man.

"You really ought to be more careful," she advised as she stepped away and returned to her phone.

"I should—you *texted* Grisham?" Disbelief clouded every syllable. "Great, but if it's not too much trouble, do you think you could, I don't know, *call* him instead?"

"You know I prefer to text."

"Yes, I know, so you don't have to talk to many people of lower intelligence. But if you could just deign yourself this once, I'd appreciate it."

When she opened her mouth as if to protest, he groaned. He'd put up with a lot and only minimal complaining, but he wasn't budging on this. Even geniuses needed limits. "C'mon, Alex, I'm not sitting on this guy until Grisham happens to check his text messages."

"Fine, if you insist."

"Uh, yeah, I insist."

She paused, then frowned as if trying to reason out a complicated equation. "Really? You could just knock him out or shoot him in the knee, and then we could…"

"No!" Cade and the man beneath him answered in unison.

Alex quirked a dark brow, then sighed before raising the phone to her ear.

CHAPTER TEN

"I really don't think they got here any sooner because I called them." Alex sniffed as she stood shoulder to shoulder with Cade, both watching as Grisham folded Tiny into the back of a squad car. "In fact, it probably took them longer because I had to explain it to him three times before he understood me. It's so hard being right all the time."

"Right." His shoulders shook with an incredulous laugh. *"I may have slightly over calculated just how fine it was."* "And I suppose you want an apology for making you talk to him."

"Yes, thank you. I accept your apology."

"That *wasn't* an apology." Cade studied her profile and the black hair whipping around her face in the cool evening breeze. "You know, you're not doing yourself any favors by acting like this."

"Like what?" she asked as she met his gaze with a blank one

of her own. No emotion, like always.

"Like this. Like you're above everyone and nothing can touch you." It was surprisingly easy to keep the frustration out of his tone, probably because Alex didn't look the least bit bothered by his words. Slightly perplexed maybe… "Like it doesn't bother you when Sarah calls you Rain Man or any of those other names or even accuses you of murder."

"It doesn't bother me."

He'd barely been able to restrain himself when Detective Walker had appeared on the scene and immediately laid into Alex. She wasn't even subtle in her insults. Alex hadn't even flinched. He'd clenched his teeth so hard his jaw hurt. "Well, it bothers me."

The rest of unspoken words dissipated in the movement and noise of the crime scene. They separated, Cade pulled away by the EMS and Alex to who knew where.

After the paramedic cleared him and a few officers shook his hand, Cade propped himself up against the alley wall with his arms crossed over his chest. A few minutes later, Alex rejoined him.

She didn't speak immediately, and he'd just about forgotten she was there when she cleared her throat. "If I let it bother me, that would mean I care. Caring is not an advantage in this line of work. It's a weakness, a defect. My brain is a machine, and I can't let emotion compromise my process."

Her words came soft and quick, and she didn't meet his eyes while she spoke. Cade made a deduction of his own. Alex wasn't incapable of caring. In fact, in the gentleness of her tone, he heard the truth. At least once before, she'd cared too much.

He'd wondered many things about Alex in the few days he'd known her—how she operated on all cylinders with no fuel, the recall of her extraordinary knowledge, if she ever relaxed—but he hadn't give much thought to what drove her. Pointless to ask really, since she'd never volunteer something like that. Just as well since he had his share of things he'd like to keep quiet about, too. And yet…

"What happened to you in that building we broke into?" Cade had watched her, even in the darkness, and had seen the trance-like state come over her. It seemed about as out of character for Alex as anything could be. Like she'd completely stepped outside of her body at that crucial moment.

"Hmm? I don't know what you're talking about."

Her denial only made him want to push that much more. "Yes, you do."

A long moment passed where neither of them spoke and both kept their eyes straight ahead, focused on the chaos unfolding in front of them.

"It was the opium, wasn't it?" Cade tried his best to watch her reaction to his question in his periphery, but his injury prevented that. Instead, he slowly turned his head to find her looking right back.

"That's really not a road you want to go down," she warned.

It was confirmation enough, though she clearly didn't want to talk about it. "What if I do?"

It might have been a trick of the light as the police lights danced across her face, but Cade thought he saw her brows raise in surprise.

"Five years ago. I hit an all-time low. I made promises to never go back. It doesn't mean I'm immune," she explained, more cryptically than he would have liked.

With her jaw set, she stared right back at him, not with the same hopeful expression she'd offered in their living room, but with the fast building walls of someone who awaited judgment. On the one hand, her history with the drug—whatever the extent might be—only served to intensify all the warnings he'd received where she was concerned. On the other, he'd never met anyone as incredible as her, and he wasn't sure her history changed that.

"Okay," he said finally.

"Okay?" Her response held a little confusion and a lot of surprise. As if she expected her semi-confession to change things between them. Cade wondered who hadn't responded as favorably as he had. Maybe the person she'd once cared too much about.

"So this case is over." Might as well make a peace offering, and clearly it was time to change the subject. "Are you hungry now? I never did get a chance to finish my meal."

He succeeded in keeping any emotion or expectation from his tone, but Alex scoffed anyway.

"The case isn't over, Cade."

"Well, okay, there's a couple loose ends, but we figured out who did it and why—"

"I figured out—"

"Fine. You figured it out, and I caught one of them. He'll

probably give up the other guy's location in exchange for a plea deal." He shrugged and stuffed his hands in his pockets. "Seems like it's wrapped up to me."

"Yes, but you're an idiot. Oh, you know what I mean. Almost everyone is. And you have to admit you sometimes fail to see the obvious. Not really your fault, but true nonetheless."

"I'm not listening to this." He pushed off the wall by pressing his heel against it.

"You're mad at me."

Her words stopped him, and he took a deep breath before turning to face her. "No. No, Alex, I'm tired and frustrated… all right, and maybe a bit mad."

"More than a bit. You're clenching your jaw like—"

"You don't get to analyze me right now." Unbelievable. "I'm going to find Sarah or Grisham and give them a statement so we can go home. And you might as well decide what you want to eat because we're stopping for dinner on the way home."

"Go ahead," she muttered absently, as if she'd already forgotten he was there. After typing a furious message into her phone, she jerked her head toward the two ambulances parked nearby. "I'm going to step outside the perimeter. Get some fresh air."

No point in replying. Instead he left her near the wall and immersed himself in the scene once again. A circle of officers gathered near where he'd last seen Sarah, so he marched in that direction. Her fiery red hair was just barely visible behind the men surrounding her, but her voice carried enough that Cade could hear the orders she barked out. Something about clearing the media and pushing back the perimeter to give them some breathing room.

Sarah Walker was impressive but in a way much less subtle than Alex. The way she took control of a situation had probably moved her up the ranks quickly. If he hadn't been privy to her digs at Alex, he might have admired the detective.

As it was, the way her face brightened when she saw him had little effect other than the slight relief that he wasn't as invisible as he felt at the moment. Her eyes darted quickly to his left and right—no doubt looking for Alex's presence nearby—before she offered a tight smile and excused herself from the officers.

"Captain Blackwell." She crossed her arms and tipped her head back to look at him. Maybe Alex was rubbing off on him, but despite Sarah's body language, he would've sworn she was happy to see him. "What can I help you with?"

"I'd like to head home, but I assumed you'd want a statement first." His hands fell to his sides as if he stood at attention to give a report to his commanding officer. When he noticed, he broadened his stance and stuck his right hand in his pocket. Much better. This wasn't the army.

Sarah blinked in surprise, then fished a notebook from her jacket. "Yeah, of course. Sorry, it's just that Holst usually disappears after a scene and shows up at the station at her convenience to give a statement. I'm not used to following the rules in cases where she's involved."

Yeah, that was him. Mr. Play by the Rules. There were probably worse things to be known as. Besides, if he partnered with Alex, one of them should be "by the book", otherwise they were likely to end up on the wrong side of the police. For science, she would say.

He recounted his story, beginning with the words painted in blood at Mason's death scene, pausing to allow Sarah to document it all. Cade explained how he and Alex had snuck up on the two men at the address, and that when one of the men attacked Alex with a knife, he'd taken him down while the other man got away. He told her where they'd found the documents implicating the men in the murders of Nathan Bishop and Mason, which Alex had said she'd given to Grisham, and how it all fit together—or at least as much as he understood.

With the recall of each detail, his frustration with Alex slipped further away as the reality of it all settled in. He contained the smile pushing at his lips only because it was inappropriate at a crime scene, but promised to give it free reign later when he walked home with Alex. The sense of accomplishment was exhilarating. Of course, she'd just remind him this case wasn't over.

"All right, I think that pretty much covers it." Sarah flipped the cover on her notepad and slid the pen along the binding. "I'll get the paperwork started on all this and call you tomorrow for you to come down and sign your statement. Nice work, Captain Blackwell."

"I really can't take the credit."

"I don't see anyone else around here who disarmed and subdued a knife-wielding maniac. Thanks for all your help. Now go enjoy the rest of your evening."

Cade scoffed as she started to walk away. "That's it? This was only one guy. Alex said there were at least three people at the scene of Bishop's murder."

"Yeah, well, I told you that listening to her would get you in trouble. Leave the savant out of this and go back to your normal life. You've already served in a warzone. It's time you sat back and let us handle things."

Anger and frustration swelled hot and bitter in his gut, and he swallowed it with great effort. No sense in spending a night in jail for assaulting a police officer, especially a woman. But he'd never understand how Sarah could continue to insult Alex when she was so amazing. Why couldn't people see that? Sure she was difficult, but her brilliance more than made up for it.

Once the anger subsided, his blood still sang with adrenaline, something he'd resigned himself to never feel at this level again.

Alex had done it. *They* had done it. Hard to comprehend what amazed him more—that she'd reasoned all this out or that he actually helped her achieve it. Sarah may have been right about him walking into another warzone, but she'd been completely wrong about how he felt about it. For the first time since stepping back on US soil, Cade felt useful, needed.

Cade scanned the small crowd of police and EMS for any sign of the raven hair and pale face of his partner. Nothing. His smile faded as more purposeful searching revealed no indication she was still around the perimeter. So much for just getting some fresh air.

He sliced his way through the crowd to stand just on the other side of the row of police cruisers and searched the few straggling onlookers. She wasn't here either.

"Excuse me." Cade caught the attention of a patrol officer getting ready to duck under the yellow tape. "Did you notice a lady about 5'8", black hair, green eyes around here? Wearing a black coat?"

"Oh," the man smiled like he knew an inside joke, "you mean Alex Holst? Hard to find a man here who wouldn't notice her."

The urge to roll his eyes was overcome only by his desire to find her. "Yeah. But did you see where she went?"

"Don't worry, buddy. She left alone." The officer lifted the yellow tape and stepped into the crime scene and winked. "Looks like we've still got a chance."

Not likely. Cade pulled his phone from his jacket pocket and fired off a text.

Where are you?

But he already knew. Alex had left. Without him. So much for being a team.

"Do you need a ride back to the Hill?" Grisham appeared outside the tape and clapped a hand on Cade's shoulder as if they were old friends. It should've been patronizing, but the detective somehow came across as genuine. Even with their limited interaction, Cade decided he liked the man.

"No, I'm fine." Cade forced the smile back to his face though the wind had vanished from his sails leaving him both literally and metaphorically stranded. Did he really want to go home and face Alex anyway? She probably wouldn't want to relish yet another victory. Instead of focusing on the one murderer they caught, she'd be more focused on the one who got away.

Wait.

She wouldn't have… Without back-up?

Actually, blindly following a savage murderer into the dark without any help or even communication sounded exactly like something she would do.

His phone vibrated in his hand. A text from Alex.

Don't wait up. I'll be late.

Late. In every sense of the word if the other guy got ahold of her.

"I, uh, think I'll just walk," he said to Grisham. "Probably grab some dinner or something."

"Sure thing." The detective stepped away and tossed his hand up in a parting wave. "Guess I'll be seeing you around."

Right. Because he was Alex's colleague now, so provided she didn't manage to get herself killed tonight, this—the cases, the adrenaline—could actually become part of his life.

But how would he even begin to find her?

CHAPTER ELEVEN

The streetlights just level with the third floor window provided the only light in the room where Alex now stood face to face with Aldrich Dieter. It wasn't much to work with, but she could make out the lines of his face, the shift of his mouth into a satisfied sneer.

"Took you long enough. I thought I might have lost you back there."

"Despite your inspired attempts to lose me, I knew exactly where you'd end up." People, even criminals, were usually so sentimental. That Dieter would return here, to his former college chemistry building, was an inevitable conclusion. As it was now abandoned and the building not scheduled for renovation until next year, it certainly didn't take much imagination to discern his location. A bit of information she'd found via an internet search and hadn't bothered to share with

Cade.

That she was alone with Dieter without any hope of someone happening by might have scared her if he wasn't so completely predictable. She was bored already. Case closed too easily, hundreds of people saved. All in a day's work.

"Well, I would've been disappointed if you hadn't found me. The great Alex Holst. A genius by all accounts, but I guess we'll see how true that is, won't we?"

Great. A show off. But this had some promise if she played it just right. "I don't need to prove anything to you. I could have the police here in minutes, and you'll be spending the rest of your life in jail. I hardly think you're worth me wasting my time."

"You're not going to call the police. If you were, you would've already done it."

True. A sound observation if a little basic.

"You want to play the game. You want a challenge."

Right again. If wrapping up this case was going to be this simple, why shouldn't she have a little fun with it? "And I suppose you think you can give it to me."

"I know I can. You're not the only genius in the room, Ms. Holst."

"So you've called this little meeting to show me you're smart. Well done. You managed to kill an unsuspecting clergyman and set up your co-conspirators to take the fall. Your poison was a nice touch, but a little elementary. Never did figure out the stable formulation, did you? I hardly think that qualifies you as a genius."

"Maybe not. But this does." From his pocket, Dieter pulled

two syringes and held them up in the dim light. "How about a game?"

"What? We both inject ourselves with your concoction and are dead before the police get here? I think I'll have to pass."

"I don't think you'll want to. You can't resist the puzzle, can you? Look at the syringes closely. They're identical in every way but one. One contains my custom blend—the kind Mr. Bishop and Mr. Mason were so fond of. The other is a potent blend of opiates designed for a pleasant high—which I know *you* are especially fond of."

Her pulse thumped hard in her neck as she struggled to keep a blank expression on her face. How could he know about that? Almost no one knew.

"Ah, I've surprised you. We're more alike than you want to admit. With a brain like ours—always racing, always on—we need something to dull the senses, turn it all off."

Don't react. Even a flinch would serve as confirmation if the roles were reversed. "I could just leave. You're not holding me here."

"You're right. You are certainly free to walk away at any time. But once again, I know you won't. There's a lot riding on this, Ms. Holst, and if you leave now, I won't be the only person disappointed in you."

She'd gotten many things right about Dieter—employed as a janitor at one of DC's largest research labs though he was probably as intelligent as any of the scientists there, a specialist in volatile chemicals, size 11 feet—but this taunting surprised her. Disappointment. That's what Charlotte always called her in that same tone. "Who else would be disappointed in me?"

"Your secret admirer. Instead of flowers, he sent me instead. Mirror, mirror on the wall, who's the cleverest one of all?"

Sweat dripped down the back of her neck. An admirer. Was it the same person who'd hired Dieter to make the poison? Admittedly, she knew nothing about the mastermind of all this. It was bigger, so much bigger, than what she'd presumed. She'd tried to explain that to Cade, but even she hadn't understood the magnitude of it.

She wasn't supposed to be part of this equation. Why was Dieter making this personal? A miscalculation. She couldn't afford another one, or she wouldn't make it out of here alive.

"Right. So you want me to pick a syringe and see if I die or just get really high, in which case you could kill me or just make off like a bandit. Sorry if I fail to see how you could possibly lose in this scenario." She sounded brave, right? Steady? She pictured Cade when she thought of that word and, for a brief moment, wished she'd told him where she was going.

He smirked. "I'll take the other one."

Oh.

A battle of wits then. She relaxed slightly.

That stupid movie Cade made her watch. The Princess something or other. Anyway, it had gone something like this. Ridiculous as it was, what if the answer was also similar? If both syringes were the poison, did Dieter have an antidote or some sort of immunity to the chemicals?

She studied the man in front of her. Sharp eyes with a dark grin. Forehead beaded with sweat, so not as confident as he wanted to appear but clearly above average intelligence. More importantly, desperate. But for what? Was it so important he prove he was smarter than her?

That answer was abundantly clear. He believed himself to be the superior intellect almost as much as she did. One of them had to be wrong, but which one?

"Stop thinking and pick your poison… so to speak." Dieter placed the syringes on a table, one near her and the other just inches in front of him.

She could do this. It should be easy. Dieter was nothing more than a common criminal with a chemistry degree, while her mind was a machine.

Charlotte's face flashed through her mind, looking down at her with piercing blue eyes as she taunted Alex. No one other than her sister had ever bested her, and Alex was determined it remain that way. For all the torment she'd endured growing up in Charlotte's shadow, she would not allow a street chemist to make her feel the same way.

Was he the sort of man who would put the deadly syringe in front of her or himself? If she could smell them, she'd be able to tell which was which, but he definitely wouldn't allow that. Besides, it would feel like cheating. She could deduce anything if she applied scientific principles. They always worked. It's what made them science.

But what if they didn't?

This was stupid. Why did she have to prove herself to him? Just go home, have dinner with Cade, and laugh about the whole thing. Grisham could pick Dieter up tomorrow and persuade him to give up the information on his boss.

Her heels clicked on the tile floor as she turned to leave, coat flared out behind her as she spun around. She didn't need to—

"Or maybe you're just not worthy enough to play with me."

Dieter's words stopped her cold. Eyes widened, fists clenched, Alex took ten seconds to force as much tension out of her body as possible. Those words had been chosen deliberately. As if he knew exactly what they would do to her. As if they came directly from her sister.

"We'll find out soon enough though, if you're worthy or not. There's something coming, Ms. Holst. Something to seek out the unworthy and lay waste to them."

His shoes made a dull thud against the floor before the hairs on the back of her neck prickled with his proximity. "Out of curiosity, which one would you have picked?"

He still wanted to play, and her defenses had weakened beyond the point of repair. Despite the voice in her head that screamed otherwise, Alex whirled on him and marched the few steps back to the table. With a steady hand, she reached for the syringe he'd placed in front of her.

"So you do think you're clever," he mused as he took his place in front of his own syringe. "You've thought it through and made a decision then. Feel confident, do you?"

"Yes." Careful not to give anything away, Alex stared him down.

"Confident enough to bet your life?" With a chuckle, Dieter flipped the capped syringe in the air and caught it in his right hand. "What do you say? Let's play the game."

No backing down now. But she was right, definitely right.

Like a mirror, Dieter uncapped his syringe and raised it to his neck while she did the same. So close she could feel the pinprick of the needle against her skin when she swallowed, but not enough to pierce the skin.

"On the count of three. Then we'll find out who's worthy. One."

Was she really going to do this? Only a 3.2% chance she'd chosen the wrong one. Cade would tell her that was still a chance she'd be a fool to take.

"Two."

She had to. This was it. What was there if not being right? This was who she was. Dieter wasn't going to take that away from her. She was right. Always right. Think, think, think!

"Thr—"

A flash of dark red splattered before her vision as Dieter crumpled forward. The sound of the gunshot reached her ears before he hit the floor. Where. Where? Where!

She leaped over the man and the growing pool of crimson on the floor to race to the window. Everything was impossibly still. Too still. Where was the shooter? With her eye nearly pressed to the bullet hole in the window, she followed the trajectory with her eyes.

Definitely not a shot from below. The angle would've been nearly impossible. So from a building of similar height, perhaps slightly taller. It'd have to be quite close as well. There. Another vacant building stood across the street and off the sidewalk a few dozen yards. At least a fifty yard shot. Statistically more likely the shot was fired from a handgun than a sniper's rifle, but she couldn't rule it out. Of course, balance of probability—

Behind her, Dieter coughed—a wet sound which confirmed the chest wound. Collapsed lung probably. Wound on the left side so likely severed a major blood vessel as well. He was dying.

But he couldn't. Not yet. She still had questions. She had to know.

"Tell me," Alex snarled as she stormed toward him and knelt to look him in the eyes. "Did I get it right?"

"Ah, so there was a bit of doubt in that great mind." He coughed again, and thick droplets of blood spattered on her hand and sleeve. "The East Wind is coming."

She started to interrogate him further, but his eyes rolled back in his head, and then he stilled forever. Both syringes lay on the floor just a few inches from her. Her hand itched to take one, to prove she'd been right, but her assumption had been based upon where Dieter had placed the two identical vials. There was no way to tell which one she'd picked once they'd both fallen to the floor and rolled together.

Heaviness settled on her as her heart slowed from a flutter and sirens sounded outside the window. Seconds later, the room was illuminated in alternating flashes of red and blue from the police cars on the street below.

Alex stood and kicked the syringes out of the way.

She would never know.

CHAPTER TWELVE

The street just outside the abandoned building had transformed from the dilapidated neighborhood it'd been when she entered to a three ring circus of police, EMS, and curious bystanders. A sense of déjà vu—well not actually déjà vu since she *had* been at a crime scene a few hours earlier—washed over her. The sirens were quiet now, but the lights still flashed and officers barked orders, probably under the assumption they'd need to organize a team to search the building.

Alex spotted Grisham almost immediately, at the front of the crowd, radioing orders and looking more concerned than she'd ever seen him—well almost. When his eyes lit on her, his shoulders visibly sagged, and he lowered the radio to the clip on his belt before he jogged over.

"Are you all right? What in the world were you doing in there?" He kept a respectable distance, but his eyes looked her over as if assessing for an injury. It was as close as concern as she'd experienced in a while. She'd tried to delete the other times from her memory.

"Don't mind the details. I've found the maker of the poison that killed Bishop, stopped a section of the city from being poisoned, and prevented the infiltration of our Department of Homeland Security. That's enough, don't you think?"

Yes, it would have to be because she wouldn't say more. Dieter had bested her, and though she felt no remorse for his death, it didn't comfort her either. Cade would say she shouldn't say those things aloud. He was occasionally right about things, and since social situations weren't her area, Alex listened to the voice in her head.

Grisham raised his brows, then shook his head as she'd known he would. He never knew how to react to an onslaught of information like that, especially when she didn't verbalize her thought process. Not that he would understand it. "But are you okay?"

"Yes, fine. Dieter, unfortunately, isn't. You'll find him on the third floor, last room on the left. Gunshot to the chest."

"That explains the anonymous tip we got then."

"Tip? What tip?"

"Someone called the station and asked for me. Said they heard gunshots in this area and needed it checked out. I just—I knew it had to be you involved somehow, so I pinged your phone."

"Of course you did." Alex resisted the urge to roll her eyes. "Well, there's very little I can tell you about the shooter other than he must be an excellent shot."

"He?"

"Yes, balance of probability suggests it was a man. Probably on the roof or the top floor of that building over there. Not that you'll find any traces of him since the place is so rundown that anyone could climb in through those broken windows."

"Yeah, well, I don't know that we'll be looking very hard for this guy. That's off the record, of course."

"Why?"

"Well, there's no one left to press charges, and we have nothing to go on. Besides, it's not like Dieter was a law-abiding citizen. This shooter may have just done us a favor."

"How very Machiavellian of you, Detective."

Nothing to go on? She'd said "very little" information. Not nothing. Already she knew the shooter was a marksman, disciplined. A shot over that distance through at least one intact window was impressive. And to discern her shadow from Dieter's... unless the bullet was meant for her. Not likely though, as only one was fired and no one had shown up (before or after the police) to confirm the kill. As far as the shooter's timing, that intrigued her. Dieter hadn't moved around the room very much. In fact, he'd been quite still. So something about the act of raising the syringe to his neck had triggered the shooter.

"Are you even listening to me?"

Grisham, apparently, was still talking to her, though she'd blocked him out as she worked through the shooter's profile and lazily scanned the crowd. Then she blocked *everything* out when one face came into sharp focus.

Cade stood outside the yellow police tape an officer had just finished stringing up.

Oh. *Oh.*

Maybe it was the distance or the distraction of the flashing lights, but Alex was mesmerized by his unassuming posture and concerned frown—frown number three but…deeper somehow. Did that make it a new one? She really had to start writing these down.

"Alex, hey, we're not done here." Grisham grabbed her arm this time and stopped her forward motion. She hadn't even realized she drifted toward Cade.

Reluctantly, she looked away from her roommate and down to where Grisham's fingers wrapped around her arm. He immediately released her.

"I'll be by the station in the morning to give my statement," she promised with her best approximation of a trustworthy citizen.

"Wait, hold on a second. You need to be checked out by the paramedics before you go anywhere. And I need every detail you can remember about what happened in that room up there."

She didn't have time for this. Another enticing puzzle already waited just a few dozen feet away. "Have you ever known me to be forgetful?"

"Well, no, but I have known you to be selective in your recall."

"Fine then, you want a statement? I followed Dieter to this building where he challenged me to a game of wits. Two syringes, one with the poison he'd concocted, the other with a high dose of opiates, which may also be lethal. He agreed to take one after I chose the other. Then someone shot him through that window up there. And that, Detective, is the truth."

Grisham studied her for a moment, and she knew exactly what he saw—someone who was much too calm for having just survived such an ordeal and watched a man die in front of her. But she wouldn't let on how shocked she'd been when the shot rang out because it would be admitting a terrible miscalculation. That just didn't happen to her.

"Okay, you can go then. I think I saw your roommate around here somewhere." Grisham scratched his head—one of his frustrated tells—then waved her off. "I'll call you if I have any more questions."

Alex weaved her way through the line of officers, conscious of several sets of eyes on her. Only one mattered at the moment. Cade shook his head with a sigh as he lifted the police tape for her to duck under.

Neither of them spoke for a moment, and all she could do was stare. Try to see all she'd missed before. See if she was right about this huge thing she couldn't explain.

Cade shifted his weight and looked away first. Somewhere in the back of her mind it registered that staring made people uncomfortable. Of course, he'd probably find that the least of her transgressions since they'd met.

"All right?" he asked without looking at her as they stepped away from the commotion.

"Of course," she answered flippantly. He couldn't know how confused she was. Not knowing his motive frustrated her, and his concern didn't help. "Just the standard battle of wits to the death, you know."

"Oh, well if that's all. Sounds like an uneventful night."

Was there anger under his sarcasm? No, just a funny mix of concern and relief. Something she didn't have much data on in regards to herself. But this was an ongoing experiment. Might as well shift the variables. "Of course, Dieter forgot one very important thing."

"And what's that?"

"Never go in against a Sicilian when death is on the line."

Cade's bright laugh told her she'd quoted the line correctly, and she was grateful she'd not forced it from her mind to make room for something more useful. Maybe making her roommate laugh *was* useful. He certainly had his utility as an assistant, and she was willing to make some concessions to assure he stayed.

How much she wanted him to stay frightened her.

Laughter at a crime scene was forbidden. Sarah had told her once in not so many words. Psychopathic, she'd said, which was, of course, wrong. Alex was a sociopath, though a high-functioning one. She'd learned the difference by the age of ten when she'd extensively researched the topic upon overhearing one teacher telling another that those Holst girls were little sociopaths.

Cade didn't seem to care about those rules at the moment. He'd caught her off-guard again. A curious man. One who struggled to follow social norms at times, yet didn't really care when she eschewed them. Sure, he corrected her when she was really out of line, but only if there was an audience, she'd noted.

Otherwise, he was likely to partake himself.

"The only thing worse would've been getting involved in a land war in Asia," he agreed with continued laughter, and she finally joined in. "I thought you said that movie was ridiculous."

"Of course it is. But with you turning the TV up so loud, I had no choice but to listen in."

"Yeah, well, you're welcome for saving your life. Just think if you hadn't seen it."

It had been so long since she'd laughed like she had with him in the past two days. Exhausted laughter that had no real reason but cleared her mind just the same. Even now, things were coming back into focus.

She chanced a look at Cade and found him looking right back at her, though trying to appear as if he'd just been noticing a shop they were passing. She was sure now. "That was an excellent shot."

A slight falter in his step was the only indication she was right, but it was more than enough. It spoke volumes about him, but she wasn't sure what to do with the information. When they'd first met, she'd deduced a laundry list of things about him almost immediately. The trace of a Carolinian accent underlying his Midwest one. Slightly raspy tone around the edges, probably from shouting orders during his tenure in the military—army, definitely—as an officer—obviously. Injured in the war and recently lost weight, so probably depressed.

All those things and so many more, but she hadn't been able to predict he would do what he'd done. She'd missed absolutely everything important.

"Are *you* okay?" She didn't look his way when she spoke this time because it might give him the impression she cared about the answer. Maybe she did just a bit, but the man *had* just saved her life.

"What?" Cade pulled to a stop in the middle of the empty sidewalk and waited for her to join him. Reluctantly she did so, wrapping her coat a little tighter around her body for warmth. "Of course I'm all right. What about you?"

"Well, you did just shoot a man."

"Yes."

Finally, a confirmation. His silence suggested no explanation would follow. She could certainly deduce one, would maybe even be right, but there were some things better left unsaid.

They fell back into step with one another, walking three more blocks until the police lights at their backs vanished.

"That wasn't your first time." Alex found sometimes that stating the obvious would stimulate a conversation from which she could gain more information.

Cade didn't play along. "No, it wasn't."

She smiled a little because she'd expected that. A glance at Cade found him smiling as well.

"I was right about your tremor, you know," she said suddenly, because she felt compelled to say something. "No way you could've made that shot if your hand was shaking."

He grunted, not angrily, and flexed the fingers on his right hand, which was—not surprisingly—unshaken. "Lot of good it does me now. The army's already said I'm useless."

"Well, it did me a lot of good a few minutes ago, so I'm

disinclined to agree with the army."

A disbelieving laugh parted his lips as he shook his hung head. When he looked up at her, his eyes seemed darker in the shadow cast by the streetlight. "You were going to take that poison, weren't you?"

Yes. "Don't be ridiculous."

"I'm far from the ridiculous one here. You like the danger, the puzzles."

"Says the man who tackled the guy with the knife."

"Don't change the subject. You like risking your life… to prove you're smart?"

It shouldn't have been a question, she was sure he didn't mean it that way, but it gave her just enough doubt to play on. "I was just waiting on you. I knew you'd follow me."

Cade didn't take the bait. "You didn't. You couldn't have possibly known because *I* didn't know if I'd follow you."

Impulsive decision-making. Not a quality she'd have expected in an army officer and certainly at odds with the caution he'd shown earlier. "But you did."

They stopped in front of their door, and Alex waited with her arms crossed while Cade fished the key from his pocket and unlocked it.

"You're really making me question my decision to shoot him instead of you," he said as he held the door for her.

Manners and a threat. What a contradiction. Or it would have been if he wasn't trying not to smile.

"Would have been ambitious of you to try." Alex breezed past him and tossed her coat onto the dining table before flinging herself on the couch. Seconds later, Cade joined her in much less dramatic fashion.

She propped her feet on the coffee table and leaned her head against the back of the couch. Eyes closed, she tried to recall the conversation she'd had with Dieter, but her head buzzed with too much information. Something about this case didn't feel finished, not really.

"He was my first Stateside."

Cade's words jerked her from her memories, and she opened her eyes to show she acknowledged him. It took a moment to reorient herself and realize he was still talking about his kill.

"Does that matter?" She raised a brow from her reclined position, afraid if she moved it might shatter the thread she wanted to pull until he unravelled before her. Alex didn't like not knowing, but this was different. Like the twist of a clever criminal or some new variable that left her racing to solve an equation she thought she'd previously mastered. Something new, something admirable and completely unpredictable.

"It shouldn't," he admitted slowly. "But I think maybe it does. I shouldn't have shot to kill."

"Instinct," she said just as she stopped herself from waving off his words flippantly. The gesture would hurt him, and she didn't want that. This was still a very precarious thread. If she pulled too hard or gave too much slack, it might fray beyond repair.

"Yes." He breathed out, his shoulders rising and falling with the exhale. "I…I wasn't sure I could do that anymore."

"Simple muscle memory. The same reason you unconsciously put your right hand in your jacket pocket but leave your left out. It looks a little odd, but it mimics the way you position your hands to hold a rifle at half-ready. And the way you notice everything in front of you—where the exits are, every garbage can on the street—but rarely pause to look behind. You've been trained to trust the person at your back. You'd like me to believe you were just a medic, that you only killed in self-defense, but that's not true either."

Cade's jaw popped.

"You're not a medic. You were a soldier—an Army Ranger—with a first aid kit, trying to put a band aid on a gunshot wound. You think that makes you a failure at both professions, but I'd argue it's just the opposite."

"Just…"

She braced herself for his anger because she'd cut deeper than ever where he was concerned.

"…amazing."

"Yes, you've said that once or twice."

"Sorry."

"No, it's fine." And it was because, as she'd told him when they first met, it was the exact opposite of the reaction people usually had. Resistance and resentment for her gifts were things she dealt with on a daily basis. But admiration? Never. It was… nice. "Dinner?"

"I'm starving. Are you actually going to eat something?"

"Chinese," she agreed. "Kung Pao chicken."

Alex closed her eyes again, and when she opened them what

felt like seconds later, Cade's hand was on her shoulder.

"Sorry, I didn't want to wake you, but the food's here, and you should probably eat." He gestured to the white and red cartons on the coffee table and the bottles of water he'd taken from the fridge.

"I wasn't asleep," she grumbled as she sat up and blinked her heavy eyes.

"Of course not." Cade shook his head and retrieved his food. He bowed his head for a quick prayer.

Silence returned as they both shoveled in the combination of rice and chicken. Alex lifted her eyes once or twice to watch Cade eat. Quick, efficient bites of a person used to eating fast before the food disappeared or the next attack came.

Normally, at the conclusion of a case, she would fall into state of boredom so severe it bordered on depression. Once or twice it completely crossed the border, and her sister had to intervene.

That boredom felt a long way off sitting here with Cade. It would certainly come if she didn't pick up another case soon, but this was a nice change of pace. She cracked open her fortune cookie and smiled. *There is nothing new under the sun. It has all been done before.*

But this *was* new. And it excited her.

"Why did you follow me?"

Cade looked up with a mouth full of food and swallowed slowly with wide eyes. She couldn't blame him. She'd surprised herself with the question.

"Because you chased a murderer, and I can't afford the rent

on my own?"

His deadpan expression didn't waver, but she cracked a smile anyway.

"Besides my share of the rent," she insisted. "Mrs. Turner's cutting you a deal, and you could easily find someone willing to live here with you."

"Okay." He smiled slightly. "Because Mrs. Turner asked me to keep an eye on everything. I think she meant you, too."

"So, you ran after me and a murderer because an elderly lady who you barely know asked you to watch out for me?" Beneath her stare, the corner of his mouth twitched and the humor bled out of his eyes. Now, she was getting closer. "You needed to save me. From myself apparently."

Because he was the soldier, and she was the warzone. It's what made the dynamic between them work.

"I'd say that's pretty much Mission Impossible."

"Hooah," she agreed.

They both shared a smile before she decided to tug a little harder. "What's in it for you? You've lived with me less than a week, and you've been shot at, done some grave digging, and had to kill a man. That's eventful by anyone's standards. And yet, you've not thought of moving out."

"How do you know I haven't—oh never mind. I'm sure you could tell from the way I brushed my teeth or handed you your chopsticks or something."

But she wasn't going to let him brush off her question. The truth was so close, she just needed him to realize it. "Why, Cade?"

He bowed his head and rolled his shoulders back. "Over there you always knew there was something on the horizon—something coming."

Alex didn't need to ask where "over there" was. Cade was back in Afghanistan for the moment, so she said nothing.

"Just a hot tension in your gut that feels a little like dread but a lot like Christmas." He looked up to meet her eyes with a sort of gleam in his own that might have looked like tears if she hadn't known better. "You knew you'd be tested, and you lived for the next challenge because that's all there was. That's all I know. And now I'm here and there's nothing."

His gaze slid from hers, but still she remained silent. Like a spider web glistening in the light, this thread was stronger than it looked.

"You…" He looked to her again with honesty shining where memories had been just seconds before. "You make me feel like something's coming."

She silently filled in the rest for him with a smile. He needed the danger, the adrenaline just as much as she did. Maybe more. Sitting in their home now, his right hand rested on his knee, his fingers still trembled slightly. When he'd held the gun, they'd been perfectly steady. This was his drug.

"Something is coming." She stood and walked to the window to peer out into the night. Her mind came full circle.

"What is it?"

Cade stood a respectable distance behind her, but close enough to remind her he was there. She didn't want to forget. It was nice to have someone at her back she could trust. Unlike him, she'd never had that luxury.

"The east wind." Dieter's last words finally came back to her, along with the feeling that this case was far from closed. Someone or something much larger still lurked in the shadows. Waiting to reap the unworthy.

"What does that mean?" Cade budged up a little closer and joined her in staring out the window. His shoulder pressed against hers, and she allowed herself the slightest press back.

"You know, I don't have the slightest idea."

ACKNOWLEDGEMENTS

There are so many people who made this book possible, that it would be impossible to list everyone who's been my cheerleader along the way. To everyone who's said a prayer, sent an email, or given me a smile when I'm feeling discouraged, thank you!

Special thanks to:

My lovely critique partners who encourage me and push me to be a better writer.

Marcy Dyer, Amanda Holland, Beth Haun, Lakin Wooliver, Salem Daniel, and Rhondia Cannon for being amazing beta readers. Your feedback was invaluable!

Brandon Daniel for his vision for the covers for this series. Thank you for turning my vague ideas into something brilliant.

Brandon Sullivan for his editing services and the verbal lashings he gave me for my comma splices. Any remaining errors are solely mine.

The Christian Indie Authors (CIA) Facebook group. This book literally would not have happened without your wisdom and encouragement. Special thanks to Heather Gilbert for introducing me to the group and being my mentor along the way.

My wonderful readers! Whether you've been with me on this

journey from the beginning or are just discovering my writing, thank you for investing your time and prayers in this project.

About the Author

Amryn Cross is a forensic scientist and author of romantic suspense novels. As a lover college football, Shakespeare, superheroes, and traveling, she is drawn to complex characters who aren't always what they seem. Her novels are character-driven stories of people who face down some of life's darkest moments and learn to reconcile that darkness with God's light. She refers to these as "between the shadow and the soul" moments. She's loved the written word from the time she was a child, convinced the squiggly lines on top of the Hostess cupcake really spelled out a secret message.

Amryn is an active member of the American Christian Fiction Writers (ACFW), The Rough Diamond Writers (RDW), and My Book Therapy (MBT).

For additional information on Alex Holst and The East Wind series and for exclusive content, visit http://theeastwind.amryncross.com.

You can connect with Amryn at the following social media sites:

- Facebook: facebook.com/amryncross
- Twitter: twitter.com/amryncross